Operation Valentine

Operation Valentine

A Hazel Oaks Resort Romance

Sarah Fischer

Kelsey McKnight

TULE
PUBLISHING

CHAPTER ONE

Nat

NATALIE KELLER CHECKED her hair for the fourth time in her bathroom mirror before finally switching off the light. Each time she'd inspected herself, nothing about her hair, makeup, or outfit had changed, but the butterflies kept her on her toes. It had been exactly nine months, three weeks, and two days since her last brief relationship had ended; before it really ever got off the ground. But she was hopeful. She believed in real love, love at first sight, everlasting love, love that wouldn't soil or tire with age, a friendship. All of it. She believed in it so much that she swore she'd never settle for less than that all-consuming love her parents and brothers had. Hopefully, she'd be on her way to it.

Nat had a date with someone who looked like he had it all together…at least that's the impression she got from his online dating profile. Chris was a high school science teacher who enjoyed walking his dog, trying new food, and learning about environmental conservation. He had close cropped hair and warm brown eyes, and his profile picture was him and a large dog sitting on the front porch of a house. She didn't know him, but she thought he looked kind. She just hoped he had similar nice thoughts about her.

She straightened her plum wraparound dress and gave her black tights another cursory glance for fuzz, then put on a pair of black booties. When she and Chris had scheduled a date, he hadn't said where they were going, which made her a bit nervous. She didn't like surprises, even good ones. She liked to know what was happening at all times, from all angles. But in his messages, he seemed so eager to take her on a nice date, she didn't want to rain on his parade. She even promised to not look up where she was going, just follow the directions.

Before she left, Nat went through her apartment, flicking off certain lights, and turning others on for when she came home later. She liked her apartment, even if some people might say it was on the small side. She was only one person; she didn't need a lot of unnecessary space. She had a large enough bathroom with enough storage for all of her skin and hair products, a cozy bedroom with a neatly made bed and white shelves full of books, a living room that was always kept tidy with a set of pristine white couches and a TV she rarely watched outside of movie nights with her friends, and a kitchen her best friend Terry would say was much too tiny for a real cook to work with. Considering she rarely cooked, this wasn't much of a deterrent for her.

Nat shrugged on a gray coat that reached her knees and

shouldered her bag before leaving her apartment, locking the door behind her. The jitters she had felt for the past week since Chris officially asked her out had turned into a case of nerves that left her heady. Thousands of *what ifs* ran through her head, some of them ending with a lovely kiss at her car and the promise of another date, and others ending with her blocking him from her phone and vowing to never speak his name again. Her nerves made her quite creative.

She followed his meticulous directions, nearing the shores of Lake George, past the Hazel Oaks Resort before pulling into the half-empty lot of an Italian restaurant. Nat was glad he'd picked something somewhat familiar to her. She'd been there right before the holidays for a celebratory staff dinner and knew she loved the food. Plus, who didn't love free bread? There was one point in Chris's favor. Maybe even two.

The night was cool and cold, and her heels made an echoing noise as she hurried toward the front door. She hoped Chris was already there so she could make a grand entrance, his eyes meeting hers as she waltzed through the door to his table.

To her surprise, the restaurant wasn't like she remembered it before. It was empty for a Friday evening with none of the usual hustle and bustle a restaurant should have. Even as she stood in the small tiled lobby, she could hardly even hear any voices, just some polite conversation coming from somewhere unseen.

A young woman in a white dress shirt and black slacks stepped up to a sleek, dark podium. "Good evening, do you have a reservation?"

"I'm actually meeting someone here; I'm not sure if he has a reservation."

She flipped open a black leather book. "May I have his name?"

Nat's heart began to pound. She didn't even know Chris's last name. To be honest, she didn't even know his first name. Was he just Chris? Kristoff? Christopher? Christian? "Oh, it's sort of our first date." She fumbled in her bag for her phone to send him a message through the site.

The door behind her opened, letting in a burst of cold air. A man that could only be Chris, as long as he didn't have an identical twin, stepped inside wearing a black jacket over a blue button-down shirt and charcoal dress pants. Nat smiled up at him. He looked exactly like his profile picture, something that soothed her, since she had heard horror stories of online dating gone bad.

"Hi, you must be Chris," Nat said with relief.

"And you must be Natalie. Sorry I'm a bit late. A parent called me today about the big spring semester project, and I couldn't get them off the phone. I hope you weren't waiting long?"

"No, not at all."

Chris turned to the hostess. "Hello, I have a reservation under Chris Thompson?"

The hostess nodded and made a mark in her book. "Of course, I have you right here. Please follow me to the private room."

Nat tried to contain her excitement. A private room? An intimate dinner over plates of lemon chicken and calamari seemed like the absolute perfect date to her. And the private room was gorgeous, more spacious than was probably necessary for two people, it was elegant with a deep red wallpaper and candlelit tables. She felt silly to have been so worried before. It seemed as if she was going to have the absolute best date she'd had in years.

"I'm really glad you showed up," Chris said quietly as they followed the hostess. "You hear all these online dating stories and wonder how anybody ever gets matched."

"Exactly! I've actually never tried online dating before, so I haven't become jaded yet. It's all about having a little faith."

"But I'm glad I had a little faith for you; you look beautiful. Even better than your picture."

Her cheeks warmed and she was glad she'd changed into the plum dress at the last moment.

When the hostess opened the door to the private room, Nat was a bit confused. She had pictured a circular table bathed in candlelight, perhaps a vase of red roses on the table to set the pre-Valentine's Day mood. Nat realized that perhaps this would be the year she actually had a valentine. It was a silly thought. Why should she be so pressed about a valentine at thirty-one? This wasn't school. But still, she longed for one. With the holiday rush over, and months before the warm weather tourists came, she finally had time to nurture some real romance. This could be the first step to the rest of her life.

But what greeted her was completely unexpected. Instead of a decadent dinner for two, four cooking stations had been set up facing an instructor. Casually dressed couples stood in front of high, stainless steel tables with all sorts of ingredients laid out in bowls and on chopping boards. There was even a little stove and a small sink for each pair to use.

"Surprise!" Chris said with a grin. "I thought it would be fun if we took a cooking class together." He shrugged out of his jacket and then held his hand out for hers.

"Oh, cooking, how fun." Nat handed him her coat to hang up with the others on a rolling rack in the corner.

What she had thought was going to be a romantic evening was now going to be a true challenge. She wasn't much for cooking, outside of very basic things. She normally ate at work, or out with friends, or takeout when she ended up staying too long at her office. Looking at the bowl of flour and whole vegetables was tying her stomach into knots. But she didn't want to be a downer. She had promised herself she would take whatever was thrown at her with full force to give dating a real shot. Now all she needed to do was not completely embarrass herself or cut off a finger while chopping an onion.

"Look, chef coats and hats." Chris was coming toward her with a pair of white jackets and fluffy hats she had seen her friend Terry wear at work. That's when she noticed the other couples were putting them on too.

Nat smiled, determined to make this date perfect. "How nice. Here, let me put yours on," she said, grabbing one of the hats and sliding it on his head.

"How do I look? Chefly?"

"Gordon Ramsey would be jealous."

"Great. Alright, your turn."

Nat tried not to cringe as he put the hat on her head, crushing the curls she'd worked so hard creating. But it was alright because he'd seen how pretty they'd looked before the hat. Why not get in on the fun? She posed, moving her arms around like she were on one of those *Top Model* shows. "How about me?"

"Prettiest chef I've ever seen."

Nat dropped her eyes, thanking him, thinking this date was starting off perfectly. Now if she could only follow basic instructions and learn to cook.

They took their places at the small counter as their instructor for the evening began the lesson. Nat tried to listen closely to the instructions as they began to make pasta and sauce, but everything was so overwhelming. She was used to cleaning up messes as the head concierge at Hazel Oaks Resort, but making sure her dough wasn't either too dry or too wet, and that the vegetables for the sauce they were chopping were the right size was completely new to her.

"No, how much salt did you put in the pot?" Chris asked as he peered into the bubbling water.

Nat looked to the small salt container. "I'm not sure; a dash?"

"No, we were supposed to put in a teaspoon, or two if we're making a double batch."

"I'm sorry, I thought he said we could just put however much we wanted in there."

Chris took a deep breath, and he looked very much like an actual science teacher she once had while living in France as a teenager. "No, you can't guess when it comes to cooking. Just like I would tell my students in lab, precision is key. For example, look at the uneven cut of this garlic. The sauce will be completely unbalanced."

"I said I was sorry." Nat's face was boiling in time with the water. She wasn't used to failing, and even when she did fail, she wasn't spoken to like that as an adult.

"It's fine. How about you just stir the tomatoes in the pot with a spoon, and I'll take care of the rest?"

Nat switched places with him and picked up the wooden spoon. The couples around them were chattering and giggling as they sampled their sauces and brushed flour off each other's noses. It didn't seem like anybody was scolding anyone else. She felt like a child, relegated to a menial task, dressed for the occasion in a too-large chef's coat and a hat that kept slipping over her eyes. All she needed to do was get through the actual dinner part, if it ever came. She was already starving.

After another half hour of almost completely silent stirring, Chris sometimes telling her to stir clockwise or counterclockwise or pause or go faster, the food was finally done. Nat gratefully took off the stupid hat as Chris plated their meals. Once their costumes were given back to a waitress, they were led to the main dining room, where their food would be brought to them to try. She hoped Chris's attitude only existed in the kitchen, and he wasn't so bossy everywhere else.

"Wasn't that fun?" Chris asked eagerly as he sat across from her.

Nat picked up one of the slices of Italian bread in the basket on the table and began to butter it. "It was definitely interesting."

"Are you buttering your bread?"

Her knife froze in midair, a pat of butter balanced on the edge. "It appears that way, yes." Nat hadn't expected to pull out her customer service demeanor at a romantic dinner. But she hadn't technically had dinner yet, and it certainly wasn't romantic.

"That's how you ruin good Italian bread."

"Really? When I lived in Italy for two years, I buttered plenty of bread and no one said anything to me about it. There wasn't even a threat of an arrest." The words came out sharper than she intended, but she wasn't going to sit there and argue with somebody about how she ate a piece of bread. It was absolutely ridiculous.

Chris had the good sense to look sheepish as their plates were placed before them. He cleared his throat as he picked up his fork. "Looks pretty good."

"Yes, very." She didn't have much of an appetite anymore, mostly because she was afraid she'd be told she was eating her pasta wrong, but she didn't slave over a hot stove for more than an hour to not try her own pasta. Besides, the sooner she finished eating, the sooner the date could be over.

"So…we made some edible food, huh?" Chris asked, seemingly attempting to lighten the mood with some small talk.

Nat nodded as she took another bite. She'd had better pasta in her life, and certainly better company. "The sauce turned out nice."

"Do you like gastropubs?"

"Pardon?"

"The restaurants where they mix chemistry and food. Make flavors into vapors, cakes into bubbles, reduce meat into foam."

"I've never heard of them." Nat couldn't think why anyone would want to make meat into foam. But by the look on Chris's face, he seemed to really enjoy it.

"There's this great place near the school I teach at. I tried to get us a workshop slot there, but they're always booked three or four months in advance. It's really a shame, since they were going to be making eggplant balloons."

"I have no idea what an eggplant balloon is. Do you tie it on the back of your chair to signify it's your birthday?"

Chris laughed, slamming his hand on the table a bit, shaking the dishes. Nat felt the urge to grab the table, hopefully preventing anything from falling over if he slapped it again. "You're so funny. It's one of the reasons I wanted to do something like this with you. You seem adventurous."

"I try to be," Nat said earnestly. "I guess that comes from living all over the world with my family. I loved getting to know different cultures and learning different languages. It's all so exciting."

"Then I can imagine living here is pretty boring, especially compared to some place like Italy."

"No, that's just the thing. I've done the traveling. I like it here. I'm ready for roots."

Nat watched as a waitress came toward them holding a small menu that she hoped was the list of desserts. She began to panic. Although she loved a good tiramisu or cannoli, she really just wanted to get home, get out of the dress, and clean the flour from her hair.

"Hi, can I interest you in anything else?" the waitress asked. "We have some lovely cakes and—"

"No, thank you," Nat said quickly, taking her napkin off her lap and putting it on the table. She gave Chris a customer service smile. "I'm just so full from dinner."

"I don't blame you. I'm not a dessert person at all."

For some reason this fact didn't surprise Nat. She offered to pay her half of the bill, but Chris stated he had prepaid when he booked the reservation. He collected their coats, leaving her to put her own on, then walked her out to the lot toward her car. When she had pictured that moment mere hours before, it had been at the end of a lovely evening, culminating in a kiss. Now a kiss was the last thing on her mind.

"Tonight was fun," Chris said as Nat unlocked her car door.

She turned to face him and gave a little sigh. She always hated this part of a bad date. "I had a nice night too. Have a safe drive home," she said and opened her car door. As she closed it and buckled her seat belt, she looked up to see if Chris was still standing there. He wasn't. He was walking back to his car. She almost got out to explain, feeling the need for him to understand her thought process. She liked rules, loved them actually, but he was so strict, almost to the point of being unyielding. That wasn't how she wanted to live her life. Besides, two rule-makers in a relationship was probably asking for a disaster. No, she needed to be with someone who had a little bit of an edge to him. If they ruined the sauce because she cut the garlic wrong, she wanted someone who would laugh about it with her on the way to get a pizza. Not someone who probably lathered, rinsed, and repeated because the bottle said so.

Maybe she'd try online dating again. This date hadn't

worked out but that wasn't the site's fault. She had liked Chris when they were talking online. She supposed real life could've been like that too. Still, she couldn't help but think being married to her job might be the closest she'd ever get. It was a good thing she loved it.

Hudson

HUDSON DOUGAL HAD stayed late at work untangling the lengths of old rock-climbing rope he'd found in a bin in one of the storage rooms. They just gotten new gear in, so he needed a place for all of the old stuff that the lodge didn't have any use for anymore. He'd been told by another adventure coordinator that he could toss everything he didn't need, but there were some good things in there that someone else could definitely use. Also, the Spartan Gym where he worked out could probably use some of this stuff. He'd check with his boss, but he was pretty sure he could find a good home for all the surplus.

He'd already found a local scouting troop who could take the rope to practice tying knots and making swings. The gym had pointed them out to him and he was only too happy to help them. Having their leader come in with a gaggle of boys and girls and matching vests, all eager to earn some new badges made him grin. He never got to participate in things like that as a kid, and it always put him in a good mood to see someone doing all the fun things he wished he could have done in his youth. Like he lived through them.

It had been past dark when he left Hazel Oaks, and he'd already had dinner in the employee cafeteria. The idea of going home to his quiet, empty apartment didn't seem like much fun. He liked his solitude as much as the next adventurer, but he liked his solitude against the backdrop of mountains and lakes, not in small living rooms with TVs and dim lighting.

He took the familiar path instead to a local gym he frequented after work on some days, since it was open twenty-four hours. Hudson had heard all of his adult life that he exercised enough at work that he didn't need to do things like lift weights or run on the treadmill. But he found that he didn't sleep well unless he was absolutely bone tired. Otherwise he'd stay up late reading or going over old maps of the woods that surrounded Lake George in search of new adventures. He just liked to be on the move.

The gym was full, as it always was on Friday nights. He went to the main desk to swipe his card and was pleased to see his friend, the gym owner, and sometimes weightlifting buddy Ben sitting behind the counter.

"Hey, Hudson. Long time no see. What has it been, twenty hours?" Ben asked with a laugh as he typed something into the computer.

"It's people like me that are keeping you in business."

"You gotta take a rest sometime."

"Yeah, when I get home. I won't stay long, just do a few reps here and there. Anything new going on?"

Ben shook his head and leaned his elbows on the countertop. "One of the trainers has a weird idea about a singles mixer at the gym for Valentine's Day. She thinks she can make some good matches. I don't know where she comes up with this stuff."

"A lot of couples go to the gym together."

"What? This isn't a fancy restaurant; it's a gym. People come here to work out and go home. I don't see you making small talk over a light press."

"That's because I'm not looking to meet a girl."

"You're never looking to meet a girl," Ben pointed out. "What happened to that girl you met at the grocery store?"

Hudson shrugged. "We went out, but there was nothing there."

"Never is."

"What's that supposed to mean?"

"You're a rolling stone, a lone wolf." Ben spoke with an air of the dramatic. "You're a tumbleweed, cannot be tamed, a—"

He thumped his hand on the counter. "Alright, alright, I get it. But you're lucky. If I had a girlfriend, you might not see me anymore. Then who would you talk to?"

"Apparently the girls at the gym mixer."

"Good luck with that."

Hudson gave him a mocking salute and made his way to the locker room to exchange his hiking pants for shorts and his boots for sneakers. Then he locked his things away and put in his headphones. Rock music blared as he stretched before going to the rowing machine. Something about the rhythmic push and pull helped to clear his mind. And he felt as if he really needed it.

He wasn't particularly stressed or worried about anything, but there was something bothering him. He felt too at home on the shores of Lake George. While most would love to live among mountains and clear water, Hudson was beginning to feel those mountains closing in on him. Things we're getting too comfortable for his taste, and he didn't like the sense of familiarity he felt while driving from one place to the other, going through his usual routines. He'd even attempted to change his routes, but there really weren't enough ways to get around for that.

There were other places he could be besides Hazel Oaks, but he just couldn't pick one yet. He could put in his two weeks and go backpacking down south for a while, where the weather was warmer. He could visit his friends that lived in Texas and see if he could get a job at a gym down there. Or, his favorite option, he could transfer to Hazel Oaks's sister resort in California.

Surf, sand, sun. He'd exchange snowmobiles for Jet Skis and ice fishing for deep sea fishing. There would be less mountain climbing and more surfing lessons. It would be a drastic change from his nearly two years in Upstate New York, but a positive one. He could get a tan, pick up some new water-based skills to add to his impressive adventure resume.

There were just a few hitches in his plan. He wasn't sure if he could get the job in California, especially not without a killer letter of recommendation from someone on the staff at Hazel Oaks. That resort was the jewel in George Sutton's crown, and he only hired the best of the best. He was good but it would take some convincing to get Sutton to see that.

As the head adventure coordinator, there weren't many people above him to ask, or at least equal to him. There was Natalie, the concierge who didn't seem to appreciate how witty he was. She could certainly write him a letter, but he doubted she would. Just the other day, he had organized an impromptu nature walk on the shores of the lake without telling her first, disrupting her very carefully planned schedule. He got more than a little talking to when he got back. But it wasn't his fault the guests had rather gone out with him instead of sipping tea by the fire or going to the spa. Sure, he probably should've given her a heads-up, but the guests loved it and that's what should've mattered.

He finished his warm-up on the rowing machine and began wiping it down to move on to the leg press. Natalie was a tough nut to crack, and he couldn't think of a way to make her love him like everyone else seemed to. Okay, maybe not love but at least not hate him. If she could just relax for a little bit and learn to let down the tight bun she always wore her hair in, then maybe she would see how writing a letter for him would be in everyone's best interest. He'd get the job he wanted, and more importantly for her, he'd be out of her hair. That should actually be the beginning of his argument.

It seemed like the perfect plan. He would find an opening to ask her about the letter and plead his case, show her how it would benefit her as well. All he needed to do was catch her in a good mood.

At that thought, he let out a little laugh. Fat chance of that ever happening.

CHAPTER TWO

Nat

N AT WALKED INTO work at Hazel Oaks Resort, pretending it was just another day in the office. Her dove-gray suit was perfectly steamed, her black patent leather heels were sensible, and her makeup was natural. Well, most of it was. Red lipstick was her signature.

The early morning light slid in through the single window behind her standard wood desk in the tiny personal office. It overlooked the employee parking lot instead of the impressive view the guest rooms had of Lake George. But she didn't mind much and put her purse in the little lockable drawer in the filing cabinet in the corner beside the fake fern. She slipped off her thick black winter coat, hanging it on the hook, the only adornment on the bare walls. Then she took a seat in the firm office chair she always swore she'd upgrade one day.

As she did every morning, she straightened up her desk, a few things partially shifted by the cleaning crew who came in some nights to dust. Nat was never one for clutter but did keep a few personal touches. There was a red-framed picture of her as a knobby kneed teen with braces beside her family in Germany and another during her father's last year with the Air Force when they lived in Guam. A third featured her and her best friend Terry at the resort on one of their monthly karaoke nights. A collection of notebooks was color coordinated in different warm shades, held up between a set of red bookends shaped like music notes. Everything had to be perfectly straight, just so.

She logged into her computer, clocked herself in, and then checked her email. Though she opened each one, she was just going through the motions, barely reading what each one said. The boss was coming in today. Not the hotel manager, the regional one, but the boss's boss's boss, George Sutton himself, the owner of Sutton Resorts.

Nat wouldn't necessarily call him an absent owner, but he lived in St Louis, Missouri, making the commute to Upstate New York out of the question. He always communicated with the general manager on the phone or through email. He definitely didn't call her, let alone schedule a meeting. Until that morning at ten on the dot. She checked her watch, a gold one her father gave her when she graduated high school. Mr. Sutton would be there to see her in an hour. Time for coffee. Lots of coffee.

Nat flicked through the last of her emails and left her office, smiling at the night shift cleaning crew who were heading out. She missed her days in housekeeping where she and the other maids would chat in the breakrooms and have informal competitions about who could sculpt what with the clean towels left on the guests' beds. As head concierge, her work kept her from forming casual relationships with the rest of the concierges. It was how she was trained even if it did seem a little cold. And yet, she looked back fondly on the days where she could gossip and trade jokes between rooms. She certainly did not miss some of the later hours she had to keep when she was new.

The main lobby was relatively quiet as she left the staff-only area and slipped out from behind the check-in desk. Many of the early bird guests would be at the breakfast buffet or taking yoga classes in the ballroom, which had a fantastic view of the rose garden. While the flowers weren't in bloom so early in February, the lush, green maze still attracted its fair share of visitors.

The main building of the resort was old, originally built as a hunting lodge more than a hundred years ago by another member of the Sutton family. The front double doors were framed on both sides by towering walls of gray stone that held matching fireplaces that crackled merrily, casting the high-beamed room in a cozy, warm glow. Everything else around her was dark wood, polished to a rich gleam. Two stories above hung a light fixture of cheerful, yellow stained glass that when on, would drape the plush, cream couches beside the fireplaces in gold.

It always made Nat proud to say she worked there. But it

was the restaurant that she really loved...and that wasn't just because her best friend happened to be the chef.

She passed the restaurant where the breakfast buffet was being served and scanned her keycard at a small, nondescript door that led to the back kitchens. It was a bustle of activity unseen and unheard from the hallway as the team continued to make bacon, pancakes, and press fresh orange juice. She scurried through the organized mayhem to Terry's small office, where the door was always open.

When Nat knocked on the wall, Terry looked up from the supply list she was reading and smiled. "Good morning, sunshine."

"Hey, Terry." Nat sat in the soft red chair that faced Terry's desk. Her friend's messy workspace made her fingers itch with the desire to straighten papers and put things away. Of course, Terry swore she knew where everything was. In her defense, Nat had never seen her actually lose anything.

"So, how was your big date?"

"An absolute disaster. We're never seeing each other again."

She frowned, an uncharacteristic expression. "A disaster? What happened?"

"He took me to a cooking class."

"And you went without telling me? You could have taken a crash course before the big day. I would have taught you a few things, so you weren't going in there completely blind."

"It wasn't my fault. The actual date was a surprise. I really thought we were only going out to dinner."

"Oh no."

"Oh yes. And he wasn't very nice about it when I messed up. Like, it wasn't my fault I couldn't convert things as quickly as he could. He's a science teacher. It ended up feeling like I was in a lecture instead of on a date." She slumped back in her seat. "I'm never dating again."

"Don't be such a drama queen. One bad date doesn't mean you have to be alone forever."

"It's looking that way."

Terry rolled her eyes. "Fine, be that way. Ready for your meeting?"

"I don't know. How do you get ready for the unknown? What if he fires me?"

She put her supply list down and tucked the red pen she was using behind her ear, the cap nestling in her dark curls. "That seems like an awful lot of work to fire one of the best concierges in the state."

"The state? Not the whole country, no, the world?"

"My mistake," she said with a laugh. "That seems like an awful lot of work to fire one of the best concierges in the world. Besides, Anna or Daniel would do it. It's why he has a general manager and an assistant. Maybe he's got a promotion for you?"

"Again, Anna or Daniel would do that. That's my point; it makes no sense why he's here." She hadn't shared these concerns with anyone yet. Saying them out loud did nothing to help her nerves. In fact, hearing them only sent her heart rate pounding. She needed to get ahold of herself. She was confident and sure of her actions. She didn't crumble like this. She took a deep breath and nodded her head, ready for whatever would happen. "I'm ready though."

"Of course you are. I think it'll be a good thing. Now all we have to do is wait."

"That's why I'm here. If I'm gonna wait, I'm gonna need a huge cup of coffee with, like, five sugars and a splash of cream."

"Oh good, everyone likes a shaky concierge. It instills so much faith."

Nat scoffed. "Actually, the coffee keeps the shakes away. It's a weird world I live in."

"Then let's get the coffee. Turn the world right."

They left the office and crossed over to the staff coffeepots in the corner of the room. It was far enough out of the way from the bustling kitchen staff. Terry kept her domain running like a well-oiled machine, leaving breakfast duties to one of her under chefs while she took on the more rigid dinner crowd who expected more than toast and eggs.

Terry handed Nat one of the nondescript white mugs and filled it up about halfway from one of the coffeepots. "Is that enough room for your sugar addiction?"

"Haha, you're so funny. But yeah, I think it's good. Thanks, hun."

"Let me know how the meeting goes. I'll be in my office

for a few more hours until the lunch staff comes into prep."

"I will," Nat promised as she added sugar and cream to her mug.

Cup in hand, Nat strolled back to her office, focusing on the wide wooden floorboards as she walked. She knew those floors like the back of her hand and the constant soothed her frayed nerves. She loved her job, made a life on the shores of Lake George in a charming shoebox of an apartment a scant ten-minute drive away. She adored her coworkers and planning unforgettable memories for complete strangers who would leave the resort with something amazing to look back on. Whatever the meeting was about, it had to go well. There was no other alternative.

Before Mr. Sutton arrived, Nat had a couple outings to organize, several reservations to make, and guests to check on. As she turned the corner to her office, she stopped in her tracks. Hudson Dougal was leaning against the wall beside the door. She groaned internally. Why was he here? She didn't have the time or patience to deal with his teasing. She took a deep breath and put on her customer service smile. This was her job.

"Good morning, Hudson. What can I do for you today?"

"I have a question about my schedule. There's a problem."

She pushed open her door and stepped inside. "Alright, come into my office and let me pull it up on the computer."

"No, it's alright, I have a copy here." He reached into the

back pocket of the dark, olive-green pants he wore and pulled out a folded piece of paper. He unfolded it, placed it on her desk and ran his forearm over the sheet, trying to unwrinkle it. After two completely useless swipes with his arm, he handed it to her.

Nat forced the smile to stay on her face, and she took the crumpled paper from him, looking it over. It was the schedule she'd finished just the day before. She read it another two times, trying to see if there was something she missed or something that seemed out of place. She didn't want to look like an idiot in front of him. That smug smile, those deep blue eyes, the hair in a constant state of disarray. He looked perfect and imperfect at the same time. It drove her crazy. No, she read the schedule a third time before looking up at him, finally admitting defeat.

"Sorry, I don't have any idea what's wrong."

"It's a pretty full schedule."

She sat down at her desk and cupped her mug. So much for a little relaxing work to take her mind off her meeting. "Aren't you a full-time adventure coordinator?"

"Yes, but I have a conflict at four I'm pretty sure I emailed you about. Can you reschedule the Johnsons?"

"No, Hudson, I need you to work. The Johnsons are a great couple, really, and they've been looking forward to taking the hike to the greenhouse before the end of their stay. I've got a little dinner basket that Terry has plans to pack. They couldn't come for Valentine's Day, so this is their Valentine's. This sunset picnic amongst the flowers with the different colors going through the greenhouse glass. I mean, come on, they have to do that."

"I got it. I'll make it up to them. I just can't do it today."

"They're leaving tomorrow at three. You don't have time to make it up to them, and this was going to be their grand, romantic outing."

He grinned widely and swiped his schedule off her desk. "Oh, I'll make the time. I'm a romance expert. Don't stress it. And if you think it's really a bad call, then I'm sure I can get Jordan to take on the extra gig. He's been begging me for more hours. Your call." He tapped her desk twice and walked away.

No, the Johnsons deserved the outing she planned for them. They were a cute and happily married couple in their forties. They had four kids and were on the first vacation they'd taken without them. The hike was one of the reasons they'd chosen to come to Hazel Oaks. Apparently, they used to hike all the time and hadn't been in forever. No. She was the head concierge, and she'd make sure they had the perfect romantic weekend. Unfortunately, that weekend required Hudson. She straightened her blazer and followed him out of the office.

"Hudson," she said loudly as he sped away from her. He didn't turn around, so she upped her pace, finally catching up to him before he reached the glass doors in the lobby that led out to the garden maze. Cold air slipped inside when he tried to escape her, but she pushed the door closed and turned to face him, lips pursed and jaw clenched.

"Look, I'm sorry about the Johnsons, I really am. I just can't today," he said firmly.

"That's not acceptable."

"Natalie, something came up and I'm sorry. I'll be here tomorrow. Why don't I take them on a sunrise hike? They can have breakfast instead of dinner. It'll be romantic. You'll be happy, they'll be happy, everyone wins."

"And what am I supposed to do with them tonight?"

"Well, see, that's why you're the boss. All those brilliant ideas of yours. I'm sure you'll think of something great. True, it won't be as good as my idea tomorrow morning, but really, give it your best shot," he said, placing a hand on the door. Then he dropped it and turned to Nat, the light smile gone, quickly replaced by worry lines at his eyes. "I'm sorry. I really am. Something just came up and I am truly the only one who can handle it. Please."

Nat wasn't used to seeing him so serious, let alone asking her so genuinely for something. She let out a deep breath, hoping some of her frustration would leave with it. "I'll work something out."

"Appreciate it. Tomorrow will be perfect; you'll be so impressed with me you'll completely forget about today. In fact, you may even be singing my name. Shall I get you some tea to loosen up your vocal cords?"

"If you don't go now, I will force you to stay here."

"Tough and brilliant. I like that in a boss. See you later."

Nat massaged her temples with her fingertips, trying to calm the migraine that was undoubtably on its way. From the clear glass of the door, she watched Hudson walking through the snow-dusted maze. And for a moment, curiosity overtook her frustration. He'd never told her what he was doing. True, it wasn't her business, but Hudson wasn't a flake. He was annoying, but he was good at his job and that was why she'd scheduled the Johnsons with him in the first place. She couldn't help but wonder what he would consider so important that he had to cancel.

Whatever it was, she couldn't worry about it then. Mr. Sutton would be there soon, and the coffee in her office was probably just warm enough to get down. Besides, now she had to plan a romantic scene to rival roses at sunset.

BY TEN, NAT was feeling much better. Terry had agreed to make the Johnsons a special five-course meal for a romantic dinner they'd share in the historic study. She'd sent her assistant Rebecca to the store to get decorations for some splashes of color and cheer for a Valentine's meal they'd never forget. She'd even called Mimi's Boutique to see if they could send over some dresses for Mrs. Johnson to pick from. Take that Hudson. She could do romance way better than him. It was a woman thing, all this romance. Guys just didn't get it.

She tried not to look at her watch as she waited at the concierge's welcome station in the lobby beside the check-in desk. Mr. Sutton was due any second now and looking at her watch wouldn't change that. Instead, she organized and reorganized everything she could get her hands on. This space was used by the entire concierge team as a way to invite guests to sign up for different activities and events, making it much less tidy than she would have liked. She added new pamphlets to the desk so that each stack advertising the local shops, the adventure activities, and the spa amenities all had seven pamphlets facing the correct direction neatly. Then she refilled the gold cup with more Hazel Oaks pens and fixed the small stack of concierge business cards. She was almost done with that when a man in a very expensive suit walked into the lobby.

He had white hair that was slicked back, a gold watch, and a big, white smile. Nat watched as he greeted everyone in the lobby, shaking hands, taking time to interact with each guest he saw. Then, he turned to the front desk and started the same thing with each of the employees. This wasn't the boss she'd imagined. He had hotels all over the country and even some overseas. The Sutton name was recognized as one of the richest around and here he was, taking time to know exactly who was working for him.

Maybe that was the point of the meeting. Maybe he wanted to get to know her since she directly interacted with the guests, ensuring they all had a great stay. It would make sense. Her nerves relaxing some, she continued to watch Mr. Sutton, ready for when it would be her turn, liking him a little more with each hand he shook.

"Who's that?" asked a voice at her shoulder.

Nat jumped. Hudson was leaning against the desk, twirling one of the pens she'd just replenished between his fingers. She hadn't even heard him walk over, let alone stand that close to her. He smelled good, almost like Christmas. Maybe it was the pine trees' scent or the light hint of snow on his hair. He was definitely in his element outside. If only he didn't irritate her so much when he was inside. She could've stayed annoyed at him, frustration oozing from her body, but she'd worked it out, and now the Johnsons would have two Valentine's Day meals. So instead, she turned to him and pasted on her smile.

"That's the boss, Mr. Sutton."

"Oh. Wonder why he's here."

"To see me."

He turned and looked at her, eyes squinted, brow furrowed. "I say this with all the respect I can muster, but why would he come here to see you? He doesn't usually come here, right? Is everything alright? Is HR involved? Do you want me to come in the meeting with you, so there's like, I don't know, a witness?"

Nat was taken aback. That was actually really considerate of him. And then she thought about what he said. Should she have contacted HR? Should she have a witness there? Maybe Anna, the assistant manager would be a good rep. Nat should've gone to her about the meeting in the first place, but she had been too wrapped up in her own nervous energy to think that far ahead. But he was right; that would've been the responsible thing to do instead of stifling her nerves with coffee.

"Natalie, you there?" he asked, waving his hand in front of her face.

She shook her head and blinked a few times. "Sorry, yeah, I'm here. Um, that's sweet of you. Honestly, I hadn't even thought of that. Let me give Anna a call. She can meet me here and—"

"Too late, here he comes."

"Natalie Keller," Mr. Sutton said, arms open upon seeing her. He immediately took her hand and shook it. "I am so glad you're here. Do you have a couple moments for us to talk? It'll be quick and then you can get straight back to work. I've heard you're quite the dedicated worker, and I'd hate to take up any time you need for our guests."

Nat took a deep breath. He'd said she could go back to work. She wasn't being fired. She could handle whatever he threw at her now. "Yes, sir. Would you like to go into the study? We're setting up a private dinner so it's completely empty at the moment as my team prepares." There was no way she was having him in her tiny, sparse office.

"A private dinner sounds lovely. But I've heard you're an

excellent concierge, so that doesn't surprise me. No, you and I can chat right here." Then he turned to Hudson and offered his hand. "George Sutton, are you a guest here?"

"No, sir. I'm one of the adventure coordinators here. Hudson Dougal."

"Yes, Hudson. Nice to meet you. Actually, why don't you stick around for this chat. Natalie may need your help."

"I'd love to, sir. I do have an appointment in twenty minutes. I'm taking a couple guests horseback riding before lunch. Will I be able to make it?"

"Yes, this will be a quick chat." He glanced over his shoulder, then lowered his voice a bit to address them. "With Valentine's Day coming up, I have a special project for, well, for you two. My best friends, Marvin and Mina Kent are coming in two days. They'll be here for two weeks and leave the fifteenth."

"That sounds wonderful," Nat said, taking a notepad out of the top drawer and then reached into the cup, grabbing a pen. She wrote down the dates and names. "We will make sure to give them the full VIP treatment. Don't you worry. Your friends will have the time of their lives."

"While normally that is all I would ask for, this is a special case. I got a call from their daughter, Louise. Apparently..." He paused, as if unsure of how to say his next words. "The Kents are not doing so well. Louise is worried they may be close to divorce."

Nat was no stranger to catering to stressed couples, but it

didn't make it any easier to hear. "I'm sorry to hear that, sir. Would you like me to book a second suite? Just in case?"

"No, the exact opposite, I want you to fix it."

"What?" Nat didn't mean to be so informal, but the single word slipped out in her surprise.

"I realize this isn't normally either of your job descriptions, but I would consider this a personal favor, not to your boss, but to me. Here's the thing. Louise booked their stay here since it's where they had their honeymoon. They also came for their first anniversary. This is a special place for them. I'm hoping you can do things, like the private dinner in the study, to get the romance back on track."

"I don't know, sir," Nat started. She loved the idea of bringing two people together, but they were the boss's friends. What if something went wrong? What if she couldn't bring the couple back together and Mr. Sutton took it personally? She loved her job.

The panic she'd felt earlier slowly started to creep back. She looked over at Hudson, trying to read him, to see if he felt the same. But that goofy smile was still on his face. She couldn't tell if he was stressed or worried or even bored. His gaze flickered in her direction. For a beat they held eye contact, then it was gone, and he was looking back at their boss.

"Mr. Sutton," Hudson began, his smile not as vibrant as before, "we are truly sorry about your friends. But what if we can't keep them together, or we make it worse?"

Mr. Sutton waved a dramatic hand in front of him, as if washing away their fears. "Listen, you two. This is a request from one man to two people. I am not ordering you to help. You can tell me right now that you aren't interested, and I won't comment on it again. If it works out, great, I'll be thrilled, but you won't receive a bonus or a raise or anything like that. If it doesn't, you won't be fired or reprimanded. This isn't official. I just…I just want the best for my friends, but I understand if you don't want to help."

Nat's heart went out to him. She had no idea Mr. Sutton had a heart like that. To be honest, she knew very little about him. But from the few minutes she'd watched him, and from their conversation, she knew she had to help him. She couldn't let him down. "Sir," she said, rounding the desk to stand before him, "I'd be honored to help your friends. Everyone deserves another chance. I'll truly do my best." She extended her hand out to him, ready to shake on the deal.

The man exhaled; his whole body instantly relaxing. He took her proffered hand and shook it vigorously. "Thank you, thank you, Natalie. You need to know I appreciate your time. I just hope it won't take away from time with your own valentine," he teased jovially.

Nat forced a laugh, trying to match his enthusiasm. She wasn't going to tell him just how single she actually was. Though, it meant that she had plenty of time to help.

"I'll help too, Mr. Sutton. I've got the time," Hudson said, the wide grin back. "Natalie and I will make a great team."

Nat's mouth dropped open before she could help herself. She quickly closed it and fixed her customer service smile back on. She didn't need Hudson's help, and she definitely didn't want it. What if he had something else to do? What if he bailed again? No, it was better she took care of things alone. "Oh, Hudson, it's alright. I have this under control. I know you're pretty busy with all of your adventure activities. I'll take care of it."

"Nonsense, Natalie. I'm happy to help."

"Right, with the activities I schedule for you to do with them."

"With the planning too. Maybe you'll need a guy's perspective."

"Actually," Mr. Sutton said, interrupting their overly polite bickering, "I think that's a good idea to get two perspectives on this. Thank you both very much. I'm going to get to know the rest of the staff but call me if you need anything at all. Have a great day." He reached into his pocket and pulled out his wallet. He opened it and pulled out two sleek business cards, handing one to each of them. "This has my direct number if there are any problems. If I don't answer and it's an emergency, feel free to use the cell." Then he waved and sauntered off, his booming personality welcoming more people as he went.

When he was out of earshot, Nat turned to Hudson. "Really, Hudson, I get that you're busy. I'll handle all of this, don't worry."

"I don't know. This could be my shot at looking good in front of the boss. I've got my eyes on a spot at one of his California hotels. This might help me get there."

"Didn't you just hear him? Helping isn't going to boost your place in the company."

"Oh yeah," he said, rolling his eyes. "Doing a favor for the boss will in no way help my career. That's probably why you don't want me to help. You want the A in the group project all to yourself."

Nat rolled her eyes too and sighed. He made her feel like she was back in high school for all the wrong reasons. "That's not what I'm doing. I'm not selfish like that."

"Besides, women don't know anything about planning romance."

Nat scoffed, tore the sheet of paper with the information out of the notebook, then slipped it back into the drawer. "Seriously? Women are all about the romance." She placed the pen back in the gold cup, adjusting it slightly so the logo would face the guests. "Why do you think women don't know anything about it?"

"Think about it." He leaned forward and lowered his voice, as if letting her in on some big secret. "In every book, movie, song, who usually has to do the grand gesture? The guy. Who's bringing flowers and setting up flash dance mobs and running through the airport before the plane takes off? The guy. Romance is a man's game."

"Right, but why does the guy need to do the grand gesture? It's usually because he's done something stupid and he needs to fix it."

"Whoa, that's mighty negative. So, I guess women never do anything wrong in relationships."

"No, actually, we're perfect. At least I am," she said primly, carefully folding her paper in half.

Hudson laughed out loud; a deep sound that echoed in the high ceilings of the lobby. It made Nat glance around to make sure he didn't disturb anyone. "Then don't you think you owe it to womankind to teach me your ways? Seriously, one day, I'm gonna get married and I'll be able to look back at this Valentine's Day and say that I learned all about love from the best. So, after my sunrise breakfast with the Johnsons, we can meet up and plan."

"Fine." Nat didn't have it in her to argue with him. He'd probably come to the first little meeting, then get bored and wander off, bailing on another of his responsibilities. It was easier to play along, but plan on her own.

"Besides, if I do well and impress the boss, I'll be on my way to California by summer and out of your hair. See, it's a win/win," he said with a grin. "Catch you later, Natalie."

Nat fought the urge to smile when he was gone. That man was infuriating, but he also intrigued her. The sunrise picnic was a good idea, more romantic than she figured him capable of. If they really had to work together, and he actually showed up when she needed him, she just hoped his one good idea wouldn't be the only one.

CHAPTER THREE

Hudson

H UDSON RETURNED FROM the hike starving. He had to get to the Spartan Gym in half an hour, but if he didn't grab a sandwich or something first, he wouldn't do anyone any good.

He pulled off his gloves, stuffing them in the pocket of his coat as he went the back way into the kitchen in search of something to eat. Terry stood at one of the long, silver prep tables chopping a tomato with the kind of skill he only saw on cooking shows on TV.

He stood next to her at the table, folding his arms in front of his chest. "Hello, Terry. Your food smells amazing, as always. Is that an heirloom tomato? Did you pick it yourself?"

She glanced up at him, her knife frozen mid cut. There was a smile playing on her lips as they entered a familiar scene. "Hello, Hudson." She dumped the diced tomatoes into a large soup pot.

"It smells so amazing, in fact, if you had anything extra

and it was immediately ready for me to carry out, I would eat it while singing your praises to anyone who can understand me through mouthfuls of your absolutely delightful cooking."

"Or, you could just chew with your mouth closed and spare us the pain of hearing you sing. Besides, if you get food on the lobby floor, Nat will be pretty upset with you."

"I think I can handle Natalie."

Terry barked out a laugh and took another perfect tomato from a bowl at her elbow. "I'd love to see that."

"No, seriously, I have to run to a thing. Can I grab something? I don't think I can make it until dinner, and I will absolutely starve to death if you don't feed me."

She shook her head and wiped her hands on the front of the apron tied around her pristine white coat. "Yeah, there are some leftover turkey sandwiches in the fridge from the Kids' Club lunch. I'll grab you a few."

"Thank you, Terry."

She got him two and he thanked her again before leaving through the storage room. He could go all the way through the hotel out the actual employee exit but leaving through the loading bay doors was a much easier way to get to the parking lot. It also gave him ample opportunities to ask Terry to feed him every time he came in or out of work. She always put on a bit of a show that she was annoyed with his endless appetite, often calling him a bottomless pit, but the smile whenever she gave him a second helping of something made it clear she loved it.

He hurried to his Jeep, turning on the heat as soon as he had the door shut behind him. He felt bad about bailing on one of his appointments, but he didn't have a choice. The Spartan Gym he went to was having a big event for some of the people competing in the Special Olympics. Originally, one of the full-time coaches was going to handle it, but he was rushed to the hospital earlier with a broken ankle, leaving his friend Ben down a trainer. Hudson didn't want to let the athletes down, so he went to fill in. He'd debated telling Nat the real reason why he'd bailed so early, but the last time he'd tried to tell her he had a scheduling conflict and the reason why, she just said his personal life was none of her business. If she didn't want to know, no skin off his nose. He'd still take care of his responsibilities.

The gym was about half an hour away, but he figured he'd use the drive to start thinking about the Kents and what he could do to help. It was winter, so that meant there were an awful lot of beautiful, outdoor activities. It'd be cold, and the couple, if they were Sutton's age, were probably about sixty. They could still be pretty spry, but maybe not quite ready for a three-mile hike in difficult terrain in winter. Maybe he could plan an easier one, then he could set a firepit for them, bring a portable speaker. Maybe he could call up Sutton and ask for a few song recommendations so they could dance under the stars to their wedding playlist. That sounded good right? The question was, would Natalie go for it?

Natalie, the perfect concierge. Everything was just so in her life, right down to the pamphlets he'd watched her arrange for the better part of ten minutes that morning. He wanted to move them so badly, maybe flip one backward just to see if her head would actually explode. She was always so put together. He didn't know why it bothered him so much. Maybe because he wasn't sure where he had a pen, or if he even owned one that he hadn't taken from one of the desks in the lobby. Then again, when he riled her up, there was this fire in her eyes that he liked seeing. She'd certainly keep him on his toes.

HUDSON ROLLED INTO the lobby after his hike with the Johnsons the next morning feeling pretty good. They were so in love it was insane. They held gloved hands throughout the hike, and they missed most of the sunrise because they were too busy staring into each other's eyes over the thermos of coffee they shared. Hudson did his best to keep quiet and act as a silent GPS instead of an instructive guide. They'd even insisted on setting up the picnic breakfast themselves. If he were to ever consider settling down, he wanted to be like them. Well, maybe not as cheesy as them and maybe it'd involve some kind of extreme sport like skiing to a picnic on top of a mountain and then skiing down a black diamond together, but yeah, like them, so in love you don't notice anyone else...or some crap like that.

But the hike had been good for him too. He'd sat on a log a distance away from the Johnsons during their breakfast and went through the photos he'd taken on his phone from the Special Olympics's event. It had been a challenge to adapt the different courses for each competitor's need. It hadn't been an actual Special Olympics event, just a bonding exercise for the participants. The organizers had said they watched all the obstacle course races on television and were interested in participating in some of the events at the gym. They'd shown up exactly on time in matching yellow shirts, ready to take on adjusted obstacle courses. Watching them dominate the monkey bars and tire flipping was pretty cool and was yet another reminder of how much he loved physical activities. They had the power to bring people together.

He picked the best shots he had and sent them to Ben so he could forward them to the families. Hudson loved being a part of the Spartan community. He'd been training since leaving high school and competing for nearly five years. He'd made friends all over the country but had yet to make it to California.

California was where his family was, the family he'd rarely seen since leaving the military boarding school he'd attended in Colorado. They didn't understand why he didn't join the family tech company, and move back to the land of sun and surf to start a nine-to-five career. He loved his parents and his kid sister, who was no longer much of a kid since going to college and getting some intense robotics degree. She was the golden child. She'd loved boarding school, accepting the family tradition of attending and learning structure, while Hudson rebelled, running as far away from that structure as he could. It's why he loved traveling so much. It brought the unexpected. Still, he couldn't deny it would be nice to see them. True, they weren't the only reason he wanted to move back there, but it was definitely a perk.

Two of the friends he'd met while training for his first Spartan race in Texas were opening a gym right outside of Del Mar, nearly within walking distance of one of Sutton's hotels. If he could snag a position there, he would have the best of both worlds: be able to make a solid living while helping out some of his oldest friends. And the Kents were his ticket to Cali. First though, he had to get through Natalie and show her he could pull his weight in the romance department.

He went into the kitchen and poured himself a hot cup of coffee, hoping to thaw his body before his meeting with Nat. He was prepared though. He'd made a list of ideas for the Kents after he'd gotten home late the night before, and he thought they were pretty great. She'd probably smile at him, the way she did when it didn't reach her eyes, the customer service robot taking over her body, and then tell him all of his ideas were garbage. But he'd keep trying. It was a challenge to him, and he never backed down from a challenge. Hudson would find an idea to crack her robotic exterior. It seemed harder to get her seal of approval than Mr. Sutton's.

After he finished his coffee, he got a fresh cup for Natalie, winked at Terry on his way out, then headed over to Natalie's office. Not that he stalked her or anything; he just noticed she usually arrived at eight thirty sharp every morning. She'd walk through the main doors, survey the lobby, and then head to her office. She was so militant. It was eight twenty-five, so he'd wait for her, look all efficient and timely in the lobby. That'd definitely set a good impression. Maybe she'd even warm to him. Who was he kidding? The woman was made of stone.

As he expected, she appeared just on time. There she was, her navy suit without a wrinkle, not a hair out of place with her fancy hair twist, her red heels clicking on the floor. She was staring down at her phone, but he knew she saw him, unless there was something else that made her stand up straighter all of a sudden.

"Oh, hello, Hudson. I didn't realize you were waiting for me," she said, putting her phone back in her overly large purse. Her red lips weren't smiling, not even the fake kind he'd grown to associate with her.

"I thought we had a meeting after the Johnson's hike."

"We do. I just didn't realize you were already here."

"As opposed to where?"

"I don't know, maybe wherever you were yesterday," she said, one perfect arched brow rising. Was she teasing him? That would be a change.

Hudson shrugged. "I didn't hear the Johnsons complaining this morning. Did you have a chance to talk to them? If not, I had them complete a survey, just in case you were worried I wouldn't give them my all." He pulled the folded survey out of his back pocket and held it out to her. Natalie didn't take it.

"Listen, my issue with you yesterday wasn't that you wouldn't be an amazing guide; it was the rescheduling, bailing last minute. I need people on my staff that I can count on. That's why this...this dual project makes me nervous."

Hudson shook his head. "Natalie, in the almost two years I've been working here, I've been sick once and I've never missed an appointment before yesterday. You can't hold that against me as if I'm this giant flake."

"Well, then prove that you're not. I mean, I checked your resume, you haven't been in one place for longer than two years since you started working. You've been here just over a year, about a year and a half and now you're itching to go to California. What if they offered you the job tomorrow? You'd leave me to handle this all on my own. So, I appreciate the help, and if Mr. Sutton asks, I'll show him surveys I've received from your clients." Then she reached out and took the survey from him. "I did get an email from the Johnsons on the way in. They said that it was a great morning, so I appreciate you making it up to them. Your idea obviously worked."

He grinned. "Hold on, was that a compliment? Are you feeling alright? Should I get a chair for you to gracefully swoon onto?"

"I am capable of giving you a compliment when you've done a good job."

"And you'll have to keep giving them because I haven't even applied for the job in California. I'd love it, but it's still in the future, so you don't have to worry about me leaving in the next two weeks at least."

Her hazel eyes flickered to the side, as if she was considering his words, then they turned back to him. "Don't you let me down, Hudson."

"You can trust me, Natalie." He held out the coffee.

She raised one brow and took it. "Then let's go. You have an hour to wow me with your ideas before I need to start my rounds." She swept past him, leaving the scent of coffee and something sweet, in her wake. Then she said over her shoulder, "And you can call me Nat."

Nat

AFTER SITTING IN her office with Hudson for an hour, all

Nat could think was how much a ticket to California was. She'd very much like to put him on that plane. His ideas, in theory, sounded great, but when you got down to the logistics, they completely fell apart. He didn't have any of the details worked out. He was the big idea guy who came up with grand schemes, then went to get coffee while the other guys were left to try and make sense of everything.

"You don't have to work out every minuscule detail right now, Nat," he was saying as he leaned back in the chair he dragged in from his office for their meeting. It balanced on the back two legs, forcing Nat to look away. If he tipped too far, he could smack his head, leaving her with a pile of paperwork about his onsite work injury, and a possible missing adventure coordinator. He was such a child some-times.

Then he stretched and laced his fingers behind his head, the muscles of his broad chest and shoulders straining against the pale blue fabric of his thermal shirt. Couldn't he get something in his size? Something that didn't look like it'd rip at any moment? How big were his biceps? And just like that, she completely missed what he'd said. She shook her head, telling herself not to focus on his looks, but on the job at hand. Unfortunately, the job at hand was giving her a migraine.

"Nat, are you listening?"

"No, I'm rehearsing a musical."

He rolled his eyes. "What we need is to go over the two

weeks broadly and get the idea of what we'd like to do. This organizing every minute of the day, man, that's so stressful. No one wants that on their vacation."

"Okay, first of all, I plan vacations for people on a daily basis, so I think I know what they like."

"But this isn't just a big vacation, Nat. This is a special trip, right? We have to wow them, and I feel like you're not going big enough. So why are you treating it like any regular vacation? It's not this paint-by-numbers trip, come on."

She slapped her red journal of menus and dessert options shut. "Excuse me, if you think I'm taking this lightly, then I don't know what to say to you. It's just a steppingstone for you, but this is my career. It's what I've dedicated my life to."

"Nat, I'm sorry," Hudson said, all mirth gone from his light eyes. "That's not what I meant. I'm just saying that maybe candlelit dinners aren't going to cut it."

"It's winter in New York, so we need to be reasonable and keep the weather in mind."

"Too bad it's pretty mild. I had this idea about taking them snowmobiling to get their blood moving, but there's not enough snow."

"Snowmobiles are not romantic anyway."

"They are if you know what you're doing."

She knit her brows and slid the journal into its place between the red and yellow ones, then took out the pink, which covered all the activities in the surrounding towns.

"That makes no sense."

"Close your eyes."

"Why, are you going to pull a quarter out of my ear?"

"Maybe later. But for right now, just listen to what I'm saying and stay silent. I want to paint you a picture."

Nat sighed loudly but did it anyway, placing her hands on the desk in front of her, fingers folded. "Okay, now dazzle me."

"Alright, you're bundled up in this frigid weather, and a man you're attracted to helps you onto this huge piece of equipment. You settle in behind him and wrap your arms around his middle before you take off across a snowy landscape. You race through the open expanse of white, diamond-tipped trees, making for a pristine backdrop to your adventure."

Nat's pulse picked up as she listened to Hudson's low voice. She had no idea he was such a poet when it came to explaining things. She could imagine the biting wind and the fingers of her gloved hands holding tightly to a parka as she laughed.

"Once he stops and helps you off the snowmobile," he continued in the same tone, "you're in an amazing clearing, a glen surrounded by pine trees. The gently setting sun is painting everything around you in shades of orange and red. In the center of the clearing is a little firepit which roars to life when he lights the kindling for you. You sit on the logs around the flame and he wraps the two of you in a blanket he brought with him. You sit by the fire, telling each other secrets, lost in the solitude of nature. Then, just as the sun disappears behind the horizon, he looks at you, claiming his view, gazing into your eyes, reminding you that as long as you have each other, you can take on the world. With a gentle kiss, he turns you to face the most beautiful sunset you've ever seen. As you ride back to the lodge, your arms around him, you feel loved, safe."

"That sounds perfect," she whispered, not even sure if he could hear it. And then, she felt his hand grip hers, a quick and warm squeeze. She jumped, coming back to reality, leaving the fantasy behind. The idea of a man, not necessarily the one in front of her, just a faceless man, taking her on that date had made her dizzy with the thrill of it. He was right, and she was completely shocked. But more than that, his hand was still on hers and she hadn't pulled away.

Nat opened her eyes and blushed, gently pulling her hands back, placing them in her lap.

"See, romantic, huh?" he teased, the playful Hudson back.

"If you're into that sort of thing."

"It looks like you would be."

"Then I guess it's a shame they can't go snowmobiling."

"I guess so."

They were both silent for a few moments. Nat wasn't sure what to say. Where was that kind of idea when they first started the meeting? His other ideas were nowhere near that fanciful, and it seemed like he'd come up with that whole little spiel off the top of his head. Part of her wondered if there was a chance she have inspired him to create his certain brand of natural magic. But then again, why would she?

Hudson turned one of the frames on her desk around. "This you?"

Nat knew which one he was talking about. She had been fifteen with braces and gangly limbs. She had a haircut the stylist had promised would make her look like Reese Witherspoon in *Sweet Home Alabama*, but made her look ridiculous instead, and the frosted-pink lipstick didn't help matters. Still, it was one of her favorite pictures. Out of all the places she lived as a kid, Germany had been her favorite, since she lived there the longest.

"Do you mind?" she asked dryly, reaching for the frame, but missing as he pulled it just out of her reach. "We have other things to focus on." The connection she'd previously thought she'd made over the idea of snowmobiling was promptly ruined by him being, well, himself.

"Not at all. Like that lipstick color on you. Very chic." He grinned and put the frame back. It was crooked and made Nat's fingers itch. "And that hair? You should go short again."

Her face flamed and she straightened the picture. "I bet your childhood photos are no modeling portfolio either."

"Oh, but that's where you're wrong. No awkward teen phase for me."

"You're lying."

His expression was one of pure innocence. "Natalie, you wound me. Would I lie to you about something so serious as my teenage years?"

"Yes," she said without even pausing to think.

"Nat, how can we have a successful partnership if you don't trust me? Look at this face," he said, pointing to his chin, turning to the side slightly. He took on the sort of expression she'd seen male models use in cologne ads, with the smoldering gaze and half-cocked smile.

She had to admit, only to herself, that he was objectively gorgeous. He had the sort of jawline and head of thick black hair that turned heads in the hotel lobby. Beneath the cavalier attitude and constant jokes, there was a handsome man. And if they'd met out in the real world, outside the bubble of Hazel Oaks where he maybe wasn't some wild jokester, she'd definitely be interested in him. But they were where they were and he was who he was, which to put it mildly, was a pain in her neck.

Nat straightened the frame. "Everyone has an awkward phase."

"I'll have you know," he began, reaching out to shift the picture slightly to the side, "I had the Shawn Hunter hair special. You know, the notorious bad boy from *Boy Meets World*?"

"Am I supposed to be impressed with the fact you had a glorified bowl cut in your youth?" Too bad for him she'd always been a Cory fan. Shawn wasn't a good choice. What appeal could the bad boy with one foot out the door possibly provide?

"It was a difficult look to pull off," he told her. His tone was serious, but laughter danced in his eyes. "But let me tell you, I gave Shawn a run for his money."

"Now that we established you were and are practically perfect, I really need you to focus. I was thinking we should—" Hudson's cell phone ringing caught her off guard, and he glanced down at the screen.

"Sorry, gotta take this," he said before answering. "Hello? Hey, how's it goin'?"

Nat turned back to her computer, where she had a spreadsheet open, and continued filling in the time slots for the Kents' stay. Hudson was having a lovely conversation with someone about rock climbing, which was hard to tune out. He kept laughing and making silly jokes while their meeting slowly neared the end. It was ridiculous that he was already showing her how little stock he put into planning.

When Hudson finished his call, he slipped the phone back into the inside pocket of his dark blue jacket. "Sorry 'bout that. You know Greg and Stevie Holms?"

"Yes, they come every season. Why?"

"Well that was Greg, he—"

"Wait, you speak to guests like that?" Heat crept through Nat's body as she tried to wrap her head around his words. He had asked Mr. Holms if his hairpiece made him feel younger. He joked that he should get a toupee for every day of the week.

He shrugged one shoulder. "Sometimes, why?"

"Because that's entirely unprofessional!"

"Depends on who you're talking to. Greg and I have a joking sort of relationship. Other guests get the strictly professional Hudson."

Nat's stomach dropped. It took less than an hour for any hope of working things through with him to completely fall apart, which was a shame since there was a flicker of hope when he talked about the snowmobile. "Okay, I have an idea. What if I just sort out the inside things while you just take the guests on outdoor outings? We can stay in our lanes."

Hudson seemed to consider her for a spell, his blue eyes roaming her face in the curious way he sometimes had, as if he was trying to figure out how her mind worked. "Hmm, yeah, don't think that's going to work for me, Nat. This is a team thing, so we need to be an actual team." He turned around another picture and his brows rose. "Is this your boyfriend?"

Nat snatched the picture out of his hand. It was taken at her oldest brother's wedding. It was just the two of them, her in a pink bridesmaid's dress, him in his army uniform. "Don't be gross. That's just my brother."

"So, you don't have a boyfriend?"

She replaced the frame, her cheeks heating. "I don't see

how that's any of your business."

"That's a no." Then he rose to his feet. "Well, looks like our time's up and I have a horseback ride around the lake in half an hour."

"The Kents will be here day after tomorrow, and we really need to get our act together if you're bent on doing this alongside me," she said firmly. "You can't brush this off anymore."

He paused, his hand on the doorknob. "Who said anything about brushing this off? Let's let things shake out a bit, start slow and see what the couple's like before packing their schedule."

"You know that's not an option for me."

"Nat, step away from the spreadsheet. Trust me, it'll work out. I'll call you when I'm done." Then, he got up and left the office.

Nat stared at the door long after he left. She couldn't believe how casually he took their assignment. He'd promised her he wasn't going to flake but couldn't seem to bring himself to show her the smallest sliver of drive. Usually she hated to be wrong about people, but for the first time, she wished desperately that she had been.

She opened up her favorite small black journal and skimmed over her notes. If Hudson wanted to brush her off, fine. She was used to working alone and getting fabulous results. She'd start off the Kents' stay strong with fresh flowers and champagne in their suite. They'd have about an hour and a half to unpack and relax before dinner in the formal dining room, a spacious place with wall-to-ceiling windows overlooking the lake and a live pianist. It was classic and understated on purpose, to ease them into romance. She'd instruct the musician to focus only on playing love songs.

The next day would begin with breakfast in bed, a couple's massage, a light lunch in the spa, and then, if Hudson didn't bail on her, an easy nature walk. If he did decide he had better things to do, then she could at least call Jordan and try to make his schedule work with this extra assignment. Jordan was only an assistant adventure coordinator, but at least he seemed more eager to do his job well and always took his weekly schedule without a word of complaint. She should talk to him about this project. He'd probably do better. At least she could trust him to take orders and not slack off.

She spent the rest of the morning coordinating outings and meals for her usual guests, only stopping when her growling stomach reminded her she needed lunch. She debated leaving the property for something greasy and bad for her like a fast-food burger and a milkshake, but as always, there just wasn't time to do what she wanted. That seemed to be a theme in her life. Though she wouldn't want to trade her job for anything, she still wished she had more small moments where she could unwind and relax without her mind racing with thoughts of guests and timelines. Well, something other than her daily run with Terry.

Forwarding her office phone to her cell phone, she tucked her black journal beneath her arm and left her office for the employee dining room. She had half an hour with nothing going on and she wanted to take advantage of it.

The dining room wasn't as lavish as the guest one, but it was still a lovely space with a view of the forest and a bit of the garden maze. There were a dozen or so small circular tables where bellhops, waitresses, and security guards ate off plain white china. She often ate with Terry in her little kitchen side office, but she knew her friend was off for the day. Instead, she collected her chicken breast, sautéed vegetables, and iced tea and went to an empty table beside one of the large windows.

Nat picked around the carrots as she ate, jotting half-formed ideas into her notebook as she chewed. It was really too bad it was a fairly mild winter. If there had been the usual amount of pristine snow coverage around Lake George, she could schedule sleigh rides and ice-skating lessons for them, and going out on the trails with snowshoes. Instead, she needed to focus on what she could plan for indoors. Although, there was a man-made skating rink in the next town over, so she made a note to check into it.

So far, she had dance lessons, something romantic but fun, maybe salsa, a private cooking lesson with Terry, artisanal hot chocolate beneath the stars where they would be nestled in a cozy portion of the maze, and a trip to the historic town of Saratoga. She underlined her favorite ideas with her pen, frowning when one of the lines wavered.

"What's with the long face? Miss me already?" asked a voice above her.

Nat jumped, dropping her fork with a clatter on the half-empty plate. "Hudson, why are you here?"

"If you checked the very specific and firm schedule you made me for today, that I've been following to the millisecond, you'd know I'm on a lunch break." He sat down across from her, his tray laden heavy with pasta, bread, and steamed vegetables.

"Sorry, I was expecting a call."

"Right, I just didn't expect you in the dining room. Don't you normally eat with Terry?"

"She's off today, but how did you know that?"

"I've seen you around, besides, Terry loves me." He grinned when she gave him a look that she hoped made her annoyance clear. "Don't be jealous, it's more of an older sister type relationship where I tease her, she feeds me, I praise her, and then we go about our day."

She hummed, looking back down at her list. She couldn't let Hudson derail her working lunch. Would the Kents be interested in a cave tour? There was a naturally formed cave not too far away that she scheduled tours with sometimes. It was really interesting to see the way the earth had been shaped, stalactites and stalagmites reaching toward each other. She couldn't recall what kind of minerals were nestled in the walls either, but the one time she'd gone, they'd sparkled brilliantly in the light from the headlamps they all wore.

"Did you just write *cave tour* on that list?" Hudson asked incredulously.

"Didn't your mother ever tell you it's rude to read people's private things?"

"She probably would have if I hadn't been shipped off to boarding school the moment I learned to talk."

He'd said it so casually, she wasn't really sure if he was joking or not. Usually, she was wonderful at gleaning truths from lies, but sometimes Hudson threw her off. "Well…still, it's rude."

"Noted. But I already know what the paper says, so let's just pretend you let me read it so we can get straight to the point."

She shut the notebook and looked at him, watching as he took another bite of his food. "Okay, what's the point?"

"The point is taking them to see the cave is a really cool idea. I'm honestly shocked you came up with it."

Nat wrinkled her nose. "If that was meant to be a compliment, it came off terribly."

"No, I mean it. People love exploring places like that. It's somewhere you can be together, doing something, but without the pressure to talk, since everything sounds so much louder in there. An activity like that is probably just what the Kents need when we start out Operation Valentine."

"Operation Valentine?" she echoed, halfway to a laugh. A day of working with him on something and things were already so far off the rails. Of course, he gave the entire thing a silly name.

"It's what I'm calling it. Makes it sound a lot cooler than Operation Get Those Married People to Stay Married so the Boss Won't Fire Us."

"Charming," Nat said, pursing her lips. She needed another cup of coffee and the organized comfort of her office.

"I always am."

"I'll finalize tomorrow night's schedule and email it to you."

He grimaced. "Ooh, not good, Nat. Can't reach me by email."

"There's a computer in your office."

"You know I'm never there. It's just a holding cell for paperwork I usually have Jordan take care of."

"Then you can read it on your phone."

"Yeah, that's not going to happen either."

"And why not?"

"Horse stepped on my phone."

Nat resisted the urge to roll her eyes. His life was a comedy of errors. Had he always been like this and she never noticed, or was this all new behavior just to drive her up a wall? It had to be the latter.

"Fine," she said evenly, standing up and taking hold of

her tray. "I'll print out a copy and put it in the adventure coordinator office. You will have to stop in for a moment. Will that be too much to ask?"

"Only if it were anyone else doing the asking. See you later."

She nodded goodbye and went to take her tray to the cleaning station. Then she filled up a mug of coffee to take back to her office. The phrase Operation Valentine rolled around her head as she walked. She hated to admit it, but it was clever, something cheeky to use when talking about it so no one would know about their secret project. But she'd never admit it to Hudson, over her dead body.

CHAPTER FOUR

Hudson

H UDSON READ OVER the crisp itinerary Nat had left on his desk for the fourth time since checking into work on the day of the Kents' arrival. He'd been surprised he'd found it among the stacks of blank waivers, equipment maintenance orders, and flyers for an upcoming Spartan race he'd be competing in. But there the paper was in all its itemized glory.

4-4:10 pm: Kents arrive in hotel lobby

4:10-4:20 pm: John checks Kents in (Natalie meets them to assist)

4:20-4:25 pm: Kents are taken to their suite (Natalie accompanies them with bellhop)

4:25-4:40 pm: Natalie explains the evening's schedule and answers questions

4:40-4:50 pm: Kents are offered champagne on ice

Hudson folded the paper up and stuffed it into the back

pocket of his jeans before finishing it. Just looking at time divvied up in slivers like that made him feel so restricted. How did Natalie plan things like that? What if someone had to go to the bathroom? Would that throw everything off-balance? Would her head spin around then explode like a malfunctioning robot?

He shook his head and collected the tote bags he had stored beneath his desk. Each was heavy with things to spice up the Kents' rooms. He'd done a little digging online about the targets of Operation Valentine and knew he had some extras that were sure to bring the romance. Through a few news articles and a big magazine spread about Dr. Mina Kent balancing motherhood with life as a pediatric surgeon, he'd learned a lot. And on a brief phone call with Mr. Sutton, he gleaned a little more.

He now knew Mina had her coffee in the morning with French vanilla creamer, and her husband Marvin liked to fish but sucked at it. They'd lived in Missouri most of their married life before moving to Texas to retire and be closer to Louise. While there, Mina had taken up gardening and Marvin had found a love for Southern bar-be-que.

As he left his office for the suite, he nearly felt guilty about going behind Nat's back to get some insider infor-mation. But he couldn't risk her saying extras weren't part of her rigid plans. So, he made an executive decision to do things his way and risk her being peeved. He did hope it would show Nat he wasn't some poor loser who shirked all of his responsibilities. And more so, he would show her he certainly did know a thing or two about real romance.

The lobby was busy with families checking in, and Hudson walked along the edge of the room to go to the massive staircase that led upstairs. He could have taken the elevator, but he didn't want to chance getting sidetracked by another guest on his way to take care of phase one of his plan.

He wandered down the third-floor corridor, keeping an eye out for a housekeeping cart. He spied one coming out of a room, being pushed by a maid named Wanda. She smiled when she spotted him.

"Hey, Hudson. What are you doing up here?" she asked, leaning against her cart. "You never venture this far into the lodge.

"Secret mission, Wanda, but I sure could use your help."

"With what?" Her voice was hesitant, wary. Why did people always sound like that when he asked them for a favor?

"I need to get into the Lake View Suite."

"Why?"

He glanced around the empty hallway and dropped his voice a bit. "The big boss was here the other day and gave me and Natalie a project. Long story short, he has some of his best friends staying in that room for two weeks and I need to set a few things up."

"This isn't going to get me in trouble, is it?"

"Wanda, come on, I wouldn't get you in trouble," he

cajoled, flashing her a grin. "You know you're my favorite. All I need you to do is swipe your keycard and forget this entire conversation ever happened."

She laughed. "If you were older, I'd make you into an honest man, Hudson. Then I'd make you sweet talk me all night."

"Wanda, don't crush my spirits, telling me we can never be together." He dropped one of the duffel bags and grabbed at his heart, falling against the wall.

"Oh, alright, enough with the dramatics. I'll help you this time." She turned the cart around to head back down the hall. "But if you're up to any funny business, I'm not lying for you."

"You're the best. I owe you."

Wanda stopped before the last door on the floor. With a swipe of her card and a click of the lock, it swung open. Hudson thanked her again and slipped inside before he could be spotted. Then, with only ten minutes before the Kents were due to arrive, he got to work.

The Lake View Suite was just as the name suggested, a lavish miniature apartment overlooking the water below, with the added bonus of a private balcony. There was a living room with plush, forest-green furniture, a kitchenette, a massive marble bathroom, and a bedroom with a bed big enough to really stretch out in. It was rustic with exposed wood walls and the dark furniture, but it had the creature comforts of any five-star hotel, like flat-screen televisions and sleek chrome appliances.

He began taking the things from his bag one by one, milling through the suite to find the perfect places for them. The potted purple violets with lavender strands for peace and calming he picked up at a garden center went on the nightstand and a trio of artisanal hot sauces from some place in Houston were put on the polished wood countertop of the kitchen. The chocolate-covered strawberries he'd had one of the chefs make went into the fridge. After taking care of a few other things, he turned on some music, old 70's hits he wasn't familiar with, but Mr. Sutton promised the pair would love.

The sound of muffled voices drawing near made him cringe. He glanced at the clock to see Nat was actually ahead of schedule. How did that happen? She was always exactly on time. For a split second, he debated hiding in one of the closets and sneaking out when the Kents went to dinner but knew that was stupid. Besides, the lock clicked, and the door swung open. He was out of time.

"You'll have a gorgeous view of the lake," Nat was saying as she stepped inside, followed by a couple in their late fifties or early sixties. Nat's smile faltered when her hazel gaze swept over Hudson and he gave a small wave.

"Hello," he said, half hiding the tote bag behind his back. "I'm Hudson Dougal, and I'll be your adventure coordinator for the duration of your stay." He shook hands with Mr. and Dr. Kent, avoiding Nat's fiery glare. She was looking at him like he just tossed the Kents' luggage straight through the balcony's glass doors.

But Nat regained her composure and swept past Hudson to the kitchenette, holding a welcome basket with a bottle of champagne, two glasses, and assorted cheeses and fruits with roses in full bloom tucked between the offerings. She heaved it onto the counter and gave the bottles of sauce a sidelong glance. "Would you like me to open the champagne for you?" she asked the Kents evenly.

"No, thank you," Mina answered, shrugging off her coat and dropping it over the back of the couch. She was a slight woman with angular features and a dark bob streaked with gray. She wasn't smiling. In fact, she merely looked tired.

"We'll worry about that later," added Marvin. He was rounder than his wife, balding and red-cheeked. But he didn't look pleased to be in the Lake View Suite either.

Then Mina opened the door to the bedroom and said over her shoulder, "What lovely violets."

"They're for you, ma'am," Hudson said, bubbling with pleasure at the faint sound of joy in her voice.

She turned to him, a small smile on her lips. "Let me guess. George told you?"

"A man never reveals his secrets," he replied seriously.

Marvin clapped him on the back. "And I see some of my favorite sauces. I tell you, if this is how the rest of the trip is going to be, it might not be so bad."

Hudson was fit to burst. He'd been with the Kents for

only a few minutes and already had brightened their mood. He dared a look in Nat's direction to see the same polite smile on her face. He couldn't see past the mask if she was impressed, annoyed, or just plain angry. Knowing her, it was probably a heady cocktail of all three.

"If there's nothing else, we'll leave you to settle in now." Nat slipped a piece of paper out of the red folder she held and handed it to Mina. "Here's tonight's itinerary. Tomorrow's will be delivered along with your breakfast. If you have any questions at all, my number is right on the top."

"Thank you," Mina said, not bothering to look at it.

Hudson gave them a small wave. "See you tomorrow."

He followed Nat out of the room, half expecting her to spin on her heel and yell at him as soon as the suite's door was closed. But she silently walked down the hallway toward the elevator and pressed the down button. When it opened and revealed an empty space, she motioned for him to follow. Hudson wanted to cut and run, take the stairs. Being trapped in an elevator with her seemed like a dumb move, but he didn't have much of a choice.

She stayed quiet until the doors slid shut, then rounded on him. "What do you think you were doing?"

"Spreading some cheer?"

"You can't just break into a guest's room like that."

"Hey, I didn't break in. I had a key."

Her eyes narrowed. "And who gave you a key?"

"Like I said before, a man never reveals his secrets. And

why are you so bothered? They loved the extra touches. You saw how they actually smiled."

Nat bit her lower lip and closed her eyes, opening them when the elevator stopped at the ground floor. She stepped out and he trailed after her. While he had been expecting her to be a little mad, he didn't really see what the problem was. Nat was too high-strung for her own good.

"You know, Nat, I did want your approval on this, but I didn't want to risk messing with your innate need to micromanage," he said lowly, coming to walk beside her through the lobby.

She stopped and stared at him, a confused look on her face. "I do not micromanage."

He raised a brow. "You're joking, right? You schedule things to the minute."

"That's called efficiency."

"It's called micromanaging."

Nat took a deep breath and her shoulders relaxed. "I disagree, but you might be right about the little touches."

"Might?"

"Don't push it," she shot back. "Besides, how did you know they'd like all of that. There's no way you got that lucky."

"I called Mr. Sutton and asked for some personal details on the couple, how to make them more at home, what they liked, things along those lines. He gave me a list."

Nat stared at him incredulously.

"Well, that was a good idea," she managed to say before opening her journal and writing a few things down.

"What's that?" Hudson asked, interrupting her thoughts. When she looked up, he was grinning, holding his hand to his ear. "Did Natalie Keller just give me a compliment? That's like two in a week. I may die happy."

Her mouth twitched, and he thought she might nearly be smiling. "Just take it and run, Hudson."

He nodded and shoved his hands in his pockets. "Until next time."

Nat

NAT STRETCHED WHILE she waited for Terry outside the kitchen's loading bay doors. Terry refused to leave out the employee exit, saying she wasn't going to walk all the way around the back of the lodge when she had a perfectly good door right beside her office.

She had her left foot in her left hand while her leg was bent at the knee. She pulled her foot, trying to stretch her quad before their usual three-mile run. Since she was just getting Terry into running, it'd be pretty embarrassing if she was the one who cramped up.

As she continued to stretch, she thought about the Kents. Technically, her workday was already over, so she should go home and order in a fabulous meal and have a glass of wine. She had a new novel burning a hole into her nightstand, begging her to read it. But at the same time, she wanted to make sure everything went well. She had to fight the urge to go home after the run to clean up and eat before returning back to the lodge to check in on the Kents.

And then she heard Hudson's voice in her head, telling her she kept micromanaging everything. She'd never really considered what she did to be micromanaging. Instead, she looked at it as ensuring the job was done efficiently and correctly. Her parents had raised her that way. On every military base they'd been on, she'd been given lists with chores or expectations for the day, and she carried the list making into her adult life, where she thought it helped her to be a better employee, and later, a better supervisor.

But maybe she should relax a little, at least about the Kents when her workday was over. She had a team below her, a team she trained, that would be able to handle things while she was gone. They knew their jobs and her expectations well enough to not let things go to seed when Nat left the office. She decided to stop by the bakery on her way to work the next morning and pick up some donuts for her crew.

The metal door connecting to the kitchen swung open and Terry appeared, ready for their run in a pair of sneakers, leggings, and her puffy winter coat. "Have I mentioned how much I hate you lately?" she asked, pulling on her gloves and hat.

"No, I believe the words you used were despise and loathe. I appreciate the effort to mix it up."

"When I asked you to get me to exercise more, I thought maybe we'd take a Zumba class with a hot instructor and then casually drink green smoothie things at a vegan cafe like normal people," she said, starting to stretch.

Already warmed up, Nat started to jog in place. "We could still do that. I have always thought a Zumba class would be fun."

"Cool, so let's find a gym for next week that has classes so you can never torture me with running ever again."

"Running is so good for you and it helps you think, you know, just clear your mind and focus on a simple task."

"What, like not dying?"

"Whatever works for you."

A few months ago, after speaking to her doctor about her health Terry wanted to get into better shape and asked Nat for help. Nat loved exercise. She swam three times a week and tried to run daily. To her, it really was a release. Maybe it was easier to say it was a release for her mind. She didn't need to make a list about running, or look up the best running paths, or the correct way to run. Her body took over and she reveled in it. It had been her release for as long as she could remember. After all, there were plenty of paths to run on at a military base. No matter where she went, what country she was in, what language she spoke, she could always go running.

As she and Terry started on the path that would take them around the side of the lake and into the woods, Nat felt her shoulders drop from the uptight and stressed position they seemed fixed in during the day. The tension in her neck dissipated and relaxation started with each inhale through her nose, exhale through her mouth. She just knew she'd feel great after the run.

"So," Terry started through winded breaths. "What's going on with you and Hudson?"

"You know that couple I told you about, the Kents? Hudson was standing next to me when Mr. Sutton asked me to help and volunteered his services, so now, we're trying to do it together."

"Right. So, the fact that you guys are spending more time together is—"

"It's strictly work-related."

"That's a shame. He's one good-looking man."

"Maybe running is bad for you, Terry. You're clearly not getting enough oxygen to the brain."

"Hold on, let me catch my breath," she spouted, taking a few deep breaths.

They didn't usually talk much when they ran, rather, they enjoyed each other's company in the silence. Well, other than Nat occasionally saying encouraging things to keep Terry moving while Terry muttered some colorful things in objection to the idea of taking one more step. Considering she and Terry saw each other all the time, she wondered why Terry was bringing it up now when conversation wasn't exactly easy.

"Okay," Terry managed as they settled in at a more leisurely walking pace. "All I'm saying is with projects like this, there's no way romance isn't going to get mixed in. You're literally trying to reignite a spark."

"Except Hudson and I never had a spark to reignite. It's completely different," Nat said firmly. Where Terry was getting the idea that their project would somehow make a little romance between them was unknown to her.

"You're wrong there. When you two fight, let me tell you, fireworks."

"Look, he's planning to move to California soon. There's no point starting anything anyway."

"I notice you didn't object. So, you see the fireworks?"

Nat thought about what Terry had said, giving it some real consideration. There were definitely fireworks in her office with that whole snowmobile story, and she did appreciate the effort he put into making the Kents' room a little more personal. But they were still oil and water, her focusing on tasks and reason while he floated through the day. In some respects, she could recognize they were teetering somewhere between love and hate, but even those words were too strong for whatever actual feelings she had. Did she have feelings? Or was the entire operation just making her read too much into things?

"Listen, I'm not saying you need to marry the guy or even make a pros and cons list about him like we're living in a romcom. But possibly, in that regimented brain of yours, there has to be some kind of fantasy world you go to. In that world, would you consider dating Hudson, letting him whisk you off on some adventure?"

"Yes," she answered before she could overthink the image of her and Hudson racing through the snow on his snowmobile at sunset.

"Then just maybe you could consider it in this world."

"Being attracted to someone physically and for the thrill of it isn't a great way to start a...a.."

"Relationship?" Terry offered.

"Yeah. I'm mature enough to admit he's handsome and has some fun qualities, but that's not enough to really build on."

"Oh? Why not? If you think he's cute and fun, I don't see the harm in seeing where things go."

Nat glanced around at the empty lake, lit by the last sparks of daylight. "I'm not the kind of person that just sees where things go, Ter. In theory, dating someone like Hudson would be an adventure in and of itself. But on paper, our incompatibility is too great."

"So you're saying there's a chance?" Terry pushed with a smile.

"I'm going to make you run five miles if you keep this up."

"Fine, fine, my lips are sealed...for now."

Before Terry could go back on her word, Nat picked up the pace, settling into a jog. Terry did her best to keep up and Nat was grateful for the silence. But still, the peace she had longed for all day was unobtainable when thoughts of Hudson kept bouncing around in her mind, begging her to let her imagination run as fast as she did.

AFTER HER RUN, Nat snuck back into the hotel after Terry had gone to her car, promising herself she'd just sneak a peek at the Kents' dinner. It was easy to not engage, as she was still dressed from her run in leggings and her black parka with her hair in a ponytail. She would never let a guest see her in such a state.

She cut through the busy kitchen and stood on her toes to look out the circular window on one of the swinging doors that led to the dining room. Nat expected to see them gazing at each other over a perfect five-course meal. Their enraptured faces illuminated by candlelight.

But Nat didn't see a happy couple. She didn't even see an angry couple. Mrs. Kent was sitting at the table alone, staring down at her appetizer. The other place setting was empty, the wineglass not even filled. She'd gone to dinner alone, been served alone, and was now eating alone. Considering Nat did that just about every night, she knew how lonely it was. And then another thought dawned on her. How much lonelier it was when you had someone to eat with and you still ate alone. She had to find Mr. Kent.

Nat stormed out of the kitchen and went up to their room, careful to stay out of sight. She contemplated what she would say, trying to make it sound as professional as she could. "Mr. Kent, I noticed you weren't at dinner. Was there something wrong with the menu? I could easily have the chef prepare you something so you could join your wife for the remainder of the evening." Yeah, that sounded right, though, she was tempted to say something like, "Hey, jerk, do you think one of the reasons your marriage is failing is because your wife is eating alone while you hang out in the room?"

Nat took a deep breath before knocking on the door of the Lake View Suite, silently wishing she'd taken a moment to change out of the gym clothes. Nonetheless, she knocked on the door. No one answered. She knocked again. Still, no answer. Nat knocked a third time and listened at the door for any sounds of life. Nothing.

Okay, so if he wasn't in his room, where was he? Nat grabbed her phone from her pocket and called Hudson. He had apparently gotten a new one, based on the ridiculous text he'd sent her that afternoon after the Kents had checked in, teasing her about how she'd deviated from the original plan and gave the couple a fruit and cheese basket instead of flowers.

"Didn't you just leave? Are you missing me that much

already?" Hudson asked after picking up on the first ring.

Nat decided to cut right to the chase. "Do you happen to know where Mr. Kent is?"

"Isn't he at dinner?"

"You'd think so."

"What are we going to do about people who don't want to live by a minute-by-minute schedule? Should we ban them from the hotel?"

"Mrs. Kent is at dinner; Mr. Kent isn't."

There was a slight pause. "What? That makes no sense."

"Yes, I know, that's why I'm calling. I just went to their room and there was no answer when I knocked."

Hudson gasped loudly into the phone. "Do you think she killed him?"

"I don't know why I even bother speaking to you."

"Relax, I'm leaving my office and looking for him now. I'll call you if I find him."

"I'd prefer if you found him alive."

"I'm sure she didn't kill him; it wasn't on the schedule." And he hung up the phone.

Hudson

HUDSON WAS GLAD he had stayed late at work that evening. Usually he was out the door at the end of the day. But that night he had chosen to hang out in his office for a bit, at least until after the Kents' dinner, just in case something went wrong.

He checked the lobby, gym, pool, cafe, the buffet, and spa, before checking the guest study. Calling the space a study didn't seem to do it justice. It was more of a library with a high ceiling and tall, dark wooden bookshelves filled with everything from children's paperbacks to well-worn hardcover novels. There were comfortable wine-red armchairs scattered throughout the room, tucked between bookshelves and flanking the massive stone fireplace that always gave the study a delicious, inviting warmth.

While Hudson would never admit it, it was his favorite indoor area in the entire lodge. Often empty in the summer and spring months, he'd spent many hours after work and in his spare time working his way through the classic books section. He learned to appreciate the adventure in *The Count of Monte Cristo* and the dark sensation surrounding *Dracula*. For a split second when he slipped through the door and entered the cozy, yet imposing room he wondered what Nat would think if she spotted him reading an anthology of Jane Austen's works. He recalled when he discovered his love of reading, sitting in a sparse dorm room in Colorado wishing he was anywhere else. His roommate had a stack of worn paperbacks, mostly classics for one of the higher English elective courses; *Moby Dick*, *The Great Gatsby*, *Around the World in Eighty Days*. He'd picked up the first on the pile,

The Odyssey by Homer, and soon fell into the tale of Odysseus and a world just beyond his reach.

He scanned the study, finally spying Mr. Kent sitting beside the fire with a book in his lap and four more on the low table beside him. He texted Nat a picture, captioning it *proof of life*, and then waited for her response.

> **Natalie:** Well, go talk to him.
>
> **Hudson:** Isn't that your job? I do the outside and you do the inside?
>
> **Nat:** I'm in my gym clothes and just ran three miles.
>
> **Nat:** Besides, this seems like a guy thing. Go be a guy.
>
> **Nat:** Please.

It was the *please* that got him. Nat didn't usually ask for help, and she certainly never used that word when she was ordering him around. Though, he wasn't exactly sure what to say, not being one of those men who was super in touch with feelings. But hey, he had to do something. Sticking his hands in his pockets, Hudson walked over to Mr. Kent, trying to be casual. Then he sat in the stuffed chair next to him.

"Hello, Mr. Kent," he said.

Marvin looked up at him with a huge smile on his face and light in his eyes. It was about the same expression of excitement he had when he saw the sauces in his room. "Hudson, good to see you. I cannot tell you how thrilled I am to find this library is so well stocked." He held up the book, a contemporary paperback with a vibrant cover. "I haven't sat down and just read in so long, but then I find out you have the entire David Baldacci spy series. I'm thinking I may even cancel our outing tomorrow to just sit by this fireplace and make my way through them. Do you serve dinner in here? Or maybe, can I bring the book with me to the restaurant? What about back to my room?"

Hudson wished he showed as much enthusiasm about his wife as he did for some spy novels. "Um, Mr. Kent, what about your wife?"

"What about her? I'm sure there's some series in here she'd like, though, come to think of it, I'm not really sure what she reads now that she's retired from medicine. Mostly it was medical journals. Do you have any of those?"

"No, sir. I think it's just pleasure reading. But, I mean, aren't you here to spend a romantic two weeks with her?"

Marvin laughed. "Would you have a romantic vacation if your daughter planned it, paid for it, then begged you to go?"

"I see how that could be tricky, but I think Natalie and I have planned some pretty romantic events for you, starting with the dinner."

"Listen, son, I'm old. I've been with the same woman for thirty-two years. We don't need these big romantic gestures or overhyped moments. That's for the young guys." He started flipping through pages of his book, but his eyes didn't move. They stayed focused in front of him. "Besides," he started a lot quieter than he'd been speaking previously, "I don't think any of that stuff would help anyway."

"If you don't mind me asking, sir, what do you mean 'help'?"

Marvin closed the book and left it in his lap. "You don't think I see through this, this whole charade my daughter set up? We're here to give it the old college try and save our marriage. Louise is hopeful like that, trying to encourage us to keep trying. Then, out of the blue, she says she won this big contest at a raffle. A two-week stay here, coincidently enough, the very place where Mina and I had our first anniversary. It's…it's all so transparent."

"Then why did you come?" Hudson asked, and then immediately regretted it. That was unbelievably rude. Nat would've chastised him, maybe made him sit in the corner with a dunce hat or something. "I apologize, sir. That was rude of me. I'll leave you to your book." Hudson started to get up, feeling like an utter failure. How was he supposed to talk to this guy without getting too personal? He wasn't Dr. Phil. Heck, he wasn't even in a relationship. How arrogant was he to think he could fix something that he'd never really experienced himself? But before he could walk away, Marvin reached out his hand and gently grabbed Hudson's forearm, pulling him back down.

"I guess you could say a part of me wished it would work. That Mina and I could fall back in love."

"Then get into the dining room with her!"

"I'd be peachy if it were that simple. We just…with Mina retiring and me selling my consulting firm last year, it's just us. For the first time since we got married. We don't have anything to talk about over dinner besides, 'pass the salt.' Without the hustle and bustle of our lives it's like, finally, we're seeing all of these holes. For example, I apparently mumble when I read the paper. It distracts her. She vacuums the house four times a week. What is she vacuuming? We don't have pets or grandchildren. Literally, there is no reason to vacuum that much, but she's vacuuming. We sit across the table for meals and can go the whole time without saying a word. That spark, it's just gone, son. That's not going to come back because we change the dinner venue."

Hudson thought about this for a few moments. His father still worked, and his mother was still actively involved in her charity work. If they lost that, how would they feel? Would they still have that spark? His gut instinct said yes, but that might have been the wishful thinking of a boy. Still, just because they didn't have work, didn't mean they were doomed to a boring life. In fact, it was his dream to travel the world with someone one day. Since they're both retired, maybe they'd have time for something like that. So maybe the issue wasn't that the spark was dead, maybe instead it was that the spark needed a different venue.

"Look, Mr. Kent, I'm not going to sit here and give you all of my sage wisdom about women and marriage because I'm single and that would be disrespectful to you. But what I think, and correct me if I'm wrong, what I think the problem here isn't the spark, but it's your activity level. If you have nothing to do, then you have nothing to talk about. Over the next two weeks, let's give you something to talk about. Then, if at the end of this you still have nothing to say, you're still not feeling the spark, then Louise can at least be satisfied knowing you tried."

Marvin nodded his head a few times and looked down at his hands. Finally, he looked back up at Hudson. "I guess we can give it a try. I'd hate to disappoint Louise."

"I'd hate for *you* to be disappointed, sir."

"Alright, well, I'm headed to dinner, maybe I'll think of something to say."

"Find out what books she'd like to read," Hudson suggested as Marvin stood with a final glance at the pile of books.

"Seems like an alright place to start." He straightened his sweater and gave Hudson a small smile. "Thanks, son."

"Anytime, Mr. Kent."

When he was gone, Hudson leaned back in his seat and groaned. This was going to be a lot harder than he'd thought.

Nat

"SO, WHAT HAPPENED?" Nat asked Hudson as she met him outside the adventure coordinator office.

"I assume he went to dinner."

"Don't be coy. What did he say? What did *you* say?"

Hudson brushed past her and went into the office, going straight to his desk. "Don't worry about it. He's there, right?"

"Come on, I need to know." Nat craved all the dirty details. She wanted a play-by-play, a complete transcription of everything that passed between them.

"Sorry, but it's guy code."

"Guy code? What is this, middle school?"

He laughed and sifted through the messy piles of papers on his desk. Just looking at the disarray made her uncomfortable. Would it kill him to put things away in the filing cabinet or tidy up the assortment of pens, one of which rolled off one desk and disappeared behind another? If he needed her to, she'd gladly sort through the mess that was apparently his life and get him on the right track.

"Let's just call it doctor-patient confidentiality," he offered, plucking a set of car keys from the mayhem and stuffing them in his coat pocket.

"You're not a doctor."

"Yeah, but adventure coordinator-guest confidentiality doesn't exactly roll off the tongue."

"You're really going to keep whatever happened a secret?"

"I'm no snitch, Natalie." Hudson's tone was serious, but the corners of his mouth twitched.

"At least tell me if there is anything I need to know. Did the hotel do something wrong? Is there anything I could do in the future?"

Hudson zipped up his coat and then looked her in the eyes. All joking and lighthearted banter seemed to disappear as he gazed at her. For a moment, her breath caught in her throat as she watched him and waited for his next move. "Will you just trust that I have this handled? Don't you think if there was something you needed to know, I'd tell you?"

"Alright. I'm too exhausted to fight anymore with you anyway."

"Long workout?"

Natalie wished once more she'd been dressed a little more professionally. She didn't want Hudson to think her casual wear reflected her work ethic. "Terry and I go for runs after work on the nights we get off at the same time."

"Yeah, I know."

"How?"

"Me and Terry? We're like this." He crossed two of his fingers and switched off the office lights, making Nat jump. "Come on, I wanna get out of here and get some sleep. Fixing a failing marriage really tires out a guy."

Nat followed him out, taking a left to follow the long hall down to the employee exit. When Hudson turned right, she stopped. "I thought you were going home?"

"I am."

"The exit's this way."

He snorted. "Yeah, if you want to take the long way. Me? I like a good shortcut. I always leave through the kitchens."

"But then you'll have to go through the lobby and a guest corridor."

"And that's a crime because?"

"Well, I don't know. I've just always gone out the employee door. Hence the name."

He nodded slowly. "That I believe. You know, life isn't always about order and rules and structure. Or at least it doesn't have to be."

Nat looked at him again, trying to decide how to interpret what he was saying. Was he making fun of her, or judging her, or maybe offering curt advice? She didn't know, and right now, she couldn't read him. "I'll keep that in mind," she managed to say before turning to go out the employee exit. His life may have been all about flying by the seat of his pants but she liked the structure and the order. It gave her a sense of peace. Right now, she wanted the peace. The dinner fiasco was stressing her out, and Hudson's lack of candor wasn't helping. Really, standing next to Hudson wasn't helping but that was a whole other matter she refused to overanalyze right now despite Terry's words floating around in her head.

"Sure thing, Natalie. I'll catch you tomorrow."

Then she remembered the Kents had an appointment with him. Nat turned around and shouted back at him.

"You'll be here in time for their nature walk, right?"

"Of course. I'll even be here a little before my shift to make sure you see how much of a responsible adult I am."

"Oh, I know you'll be one. I'm coming with you." She didn't even know why she'd said it. She'd never gone on any of the hikes with the other guides. She really didn't micromanage this much. But with Hudson keeping Mr. Kent's secret, she didn't feel good about leaving him alone with them. Though, logically, she knew he'd probably have been fine on his own.

"Yeah, no, I don't think that's necessary. I know how to do my job." All signs of mirth had left him, his lips a firm line and his brows lowered.

Nat knew she put her foot in her mouth. She hadn't meant to offend him. "That's not what I meant. I just think it would be smart of me to go as well. You know, offer a woman's point of view."

"In case I mess things up? Do you really think I'm capable of ruining the marriage in an hour nature walk?"

Crap, Nat's mind started racing with ways to try and save this. Hudson was good at his job but his job wasn't solely nature walks this time. She wanted to trust him, no, she needed to trust him but something, as it always seemed to, was preventing her. She wanted to be on that nature walk.

"No, no, no. You keep saying we need to work together, so maybe both of us going on the nature walk will be a good thing. Maybe I'll notice something you don't since you're leading the walk. My mind will be clear and focused on the couple."

He seemed to consider this for a moment, then shrugged. "Sure, if you think you'd like that kind of thing."

"It doesn't really matter if I like it or not. We have a job to do and I'm going to see it through."

"Suit yourself. Night."

"Good night."

Nat watched him turn on his heel and begin striding down the hallway before heading toward the official employee exit. He could be terribly casual with guests, and she was worried he'd slip into his joking ways. Knowing him, he might let a crude jest slip and undo whatever magic he'd worked at dinner. Or worse, what if he and Mr. Kent were now all buddy-buddy and Mrs. Kent was left out? No, it's better that she went. Of course, there had never been any complaints about Hudson's conduct with any guest in his time at Hazel Oaks, but Nat wasn't about to take a chance when the stakes were so high. One wrong move, and the Kents could take a nosedive right to divorce court. Though, now that she thought about it, maybe she could start writing up some attributes Hudson had. Like a recommendation. She could give it to him for when he applied to California. It would definitely help him get the job. She'd tell him about it tomorrow, and he'd be thrilled she was going on the hike. Though, part of her wished he'd be thrilled just because she was there. It made her rethink what Terry had said. If he actually liked her, wouldn't he want to spend more time with her? Wouldn't he want her on the hike?

He'd balked at the very idea that she go with him. Maybe that was because she'd framed it like he was incapable of doing his job? Whatever it was, she pushed Terry's words to the back of her mind and tried to find the Zen she'd felt after the run. With that idea in mind, her body started to relax as she headed to her car.

The dark night air was cold, tasting of snow and greenery. While she enjoyed summer and fall at the lodge the most, the particular blend of scents that only came with winter was one of her personal favorites. Beneath the black, starry sky with the promise of flurries and vibrant spruce trees, it was easy to imagine a couple falling back in love. It almost made her long for someone to share in the small slices of peace she'd grown to enjoy.

But there was no time to think of her own lack of romance. She had a marriage to save and a nature walk to prepare for.

CHAPTER FIVE

Hudson

HUDSON WAS ALREADY waiting in the lobby when the Kents were due to arrive. He had a casual route for them, a stroll that would take them beside the lake and through a patch of wood where he often saw deer and other animals along the pine needle floor. Although a light layer of snow had fallen during the night, which could mean the animals would be bunkered down again. Still, the snow would be all picturesque and romantic.

The addition of Nat joining them was unexpected to say the least. He'd seen her running sometimes when leaving work or coming back from an evening hike, but she still didn't strike him as someone very nature-y. He could see her maybe hanging out by the lake, but not exactly traipsing through the trees and dodging rocks in the trails. And there was no way she did it in her pressed suit and heels.

But it wasn't just the suit that didn't exactly fit into his idea of a nice nature walk. In his opinion, Mina and Marvin needed to be in a calm, relaxing environment, and Nat's wound-up personality didn't seem to inspire leisure, even if it was a little fun to watch her unravel every once in a while. He wondered if she'd show up with a schedule for the walk. He could hear her now: "At this time, we'll be viewing the birds. Exactly three minutes after that, we'll look into the clearing for deer." He laughed a little to himself at the thought.

"Something funny?" asked a voice at his shoulder.

Nat was beside him, looking ready for a spin in the forest in sneakers, green leggings, a blue jacket, and a tan knit scarf that she had wound around her neck. Her hair was even in the same high ponytail it had been in the night before, only much neater. He'd thought seeing her so dressed down was a fluke, but there she was in the daylight, looking like someone who actually belonged on the side of a mountain. He liked seeing her like this. She was one of those women who'd be beautiful in a paper bag, but this more relaxed Nat seemed like someone he could have fun with. Maybe today wouldn't be as intense as he thought.

"Hey," he greeted. "No, just thinking of some things to do with the Kents."

She dug into her coat pocket and took out a miniature red notebook with a little pen. "Oh? What are they?"

"Do you seriously carry one of those with you everywhere?"

"I like being able to keep track of things. It's very efficient."

"Have you been this efficient from birth?"

"Being a military brat will do that to you," she said lightly, checking the thin gold watch she had on her left wrist.

Nat was a military brat? Well, that made sense. He could see her marching around as a kid, making sure all her Barbies were ready for inspection. The boarding school he'd gone to had tried to instill the same values of order and efficiency in him, but it had done the opposite. He'd rebelled against that kind of structure, so much that he moved every two years, always trying to keep his options open and avoid the feeling of being boxed in. And here, looking up at him with her clear eyes, was his polar opposite. It was almost laughable that they were in the same spot when they lived their lives so differently.

Then the elevator doors opened and the Kents appeared, dressed appropriately, but not exactly dripping with enthusiasm. They'd both shown up, so beggars couldn't be choosers, but they looked like strangers walking toward him, not even glancing at one another. He hadn't expected them to be holding hands and waxing poetic about their newly revived relationship, but it wasn't exactly inspiring confidence.

"Good afternoon," he greeted merrily, hoping some of his good mood would spark something in them.

"Hi," they said in unison, distantly, evenly.

"I hope you guys are ready to get some fresh air."

"We aren't going to be on the mountains or anything, right?" asked Mina, adjusting her pastel purple scarf.

"No, just an easy stroll. We've had a mild winter, so many of the animals are coming out of hiding early," he explained, opening the heavy lobby doors for them. "If you enjoy today, we can certainly set up a longer excursion to one of our lookout points."

"Lookout points?"

"Let's just say there's one I think you would really like but it is a bit of work to get there. Although, trust me, it pays off in the end," Hudson promised. He really did think Mina would enjoy the particular one he had in mind. It was a gem of a place tucked into the side of Black Mountain, featuring a wonderful view of Lake George via the glass of a perfectly tended greenhouse that was kept at a balmy temperature all year round. He didn't take all his guests there, but he'd certainly take the Kents.

"And I'll just be tagging along today," Nat added with a smile. Her face seemed softer, a little more open without her usual red lipstick. He hadn't noticed before how easy it was to see her displeasure for his words or actions when there was such a vibrant color to showcase his faults.

"Wonderful," Mr. Kent said, rubbing his hands together. "Let's get started." He then reached into his pocket pulling out one glove. He groaned. "Oh, I must've left the other one upstairs or dropped it along the way. I'll be right back." He turned and headed toward the elevator.

Mrs. Kent watched him go and then shook her head. She turned back to Hudson and Nat. "I'm so sorry about him.

He'd lose his head if it weren't attached." She turned back and looked at him again. "I better go help him. He can never find anything without me."

"Then I guess it's a good thing he has you," Nat said with a polite smile; the one Hudson knew as one of her many guest appropriate expressions.

Mrs. Kent headed toward the elevator, leaving him and Nat beside the double glass doors of the lobby.

Nat reached out a hand and placed it on his forearm, her red nails contracting sharply with the navy blue of his coat. "Hudson, I wanted to apologize for yesterday. I didn't mean to imply you couldn't do this job. I just wanted to do whatever I could to make things go smoothly. Besides, since I'm coming with you, I'll be able to write a recommendation about this excursion. You can use it when you apply to the California location."

"Well, actually, that sounds great. But now I'm nervous with the great Natalie Keller watching over me. This better be the best nature walk of my life. Tell me, if I do something wrong, will I be flogged or simply sent home without Terry's cooking?" he asked, teasing her. He wasn't used to her being in an apologetic mood and didn't really know how to interact with her when she wasn't being her usual, tight-laced self.

She dropped her hand and took a step back. "Forget it, I was just trying to be nice." She stuck her hand in her pocket again and then looked in the direction of the doors that led to the offices. "I forgot something. I'll be right back."

Hudson rubbed his temples as she walked away. He'd messed up yet again. Sometimes his humor was a gift, and other times it gave him a headache. Nat had apologized *and* offered to write him a recommendation, then he had to open his big mouth.

He really needed to give her a break and cut back on the teasing. She may be uptight, but she was so good at her job and cared more than anyone else. It seemed it was now his turn to apologize, his least favorite pastime.

When Mina, Marvin, and Nat had returned, Hudson led the way out the double glass doors and down the paved path that rounded the side of the hotel. It would go around the garden maze and let off near the swimming docks on the edge of the lake. From there, he would take them to the tree-lined path he liked best, the one a little bit farther off than the others the junior adventure coordinators usually used.

"How was your morning?" Nat asked, falling in beside Mina.

"It was fine. I enjoyed the spa."

She flipped her notebook open and made a note. "If you'd like, I can set up different spa appointments through-out your stay with us."

"I think I'd like that. It's been ages since I've felt truly pampered."

As Nat began listing off the various spa amenities, Hudson stepped alongside Marvin and lowered his voice. "Hey, how's it goin'?"

"It's goin'," he said, sounding a little tired, or maybe bored.

"Was dinner okay?"

"The food was great."

"And things with your wife?" he pressed, making sure Mina and Nat were still going over manicures and facials.

Marvin toyed with the zipper of his puffy blue jacket. "I tried the book thing and it didn't pan out. For the past few decades all she's read have been medical journals. I like a good spy novel, something with some action and mystery."

"Okay, so she's not a pleasure reader, nothing wrong with that. We just need to broaden things a little. How about movies? Hobbies? She likes to garden, maybe you can focus on that?"

"I already had the landscapers set her up a nice plot in the yard back home but it's not like I do it with her."

Hudson was beginning to see why the pair was struggling in the romance department. Marvin at least seemed almost apathetic to his marital issues. If books as a talking topic didn't pan out, why not go for another one? Small talk was easy, and he didn't see how Marvin had survived more than fifty years of his life without using a conversation starter like, see any good movies lately?

"You could always offer," Hudson said, deciding that bringing up Marvin's conversational shortcomings wasn't going to get either one anywhere.

Marvin nodded a little and kept walking.

The group was coming up to the lake, which was frozen, but cut with a few spidery cracks that made it clear skating or taking a tour wouldn't be a good idea. He wished it was either one or the other. In the summer, when the lake was warm and so clear he could count the smooth stones at the bottom, he could spend hours on the shore.

He'd spent a lot of the past July on sailboats with the instructor, a bear of a man named Finn, and kayaking along the coast. On some parts of the lake, there would be pockets of pure life, waterlily forests with fish and dragonflies. He'd miss the crisp, fresh water when he made it to Cali.

"What a beautiful lake," Mina sighed as they hit the shore.

"Careful," he warned. "The rocks may be slippery." Then, he had an idea. "Maybe you should hold hands, just in case."

Mina and Marvin glanced at each other like the idea would have never crossed their minds, then they intertwined their gloved fingers. Hudson shot a look at Nat, who seemed very impressed.

"Good thinking," she whispered as the Kents began walking ahead of them, leaving a trail of footprints in the pristine show.

"Not exactly a lie; it can be a little slick."

Nat's foot suddenly went out from under her and she caught herself before falling. Hudson grabbed her arm to steady her. "See? Slippery."

"If one of them falls and breaks a leg, Mr. Sutton won't be pleased," she said, the previous flash of humor gone from her voice.

"I've never lost a guest, Nat. And look, they're holding tight to each other. I did good."

Mina was leaning heavily on Marvin as they walked, each pointing out stones to the other and telling them to watch their step. While they could seem distant, it was still clear they cared about each other's well-being.

"Then I guess you can let go of me," Nat said, looking down at his hand.

"I don't know. Maybe you'll be the one to break my prefect record. Besides, I told them to hold on to each other. Wouldn't it make sense if we did too?"

She stared up at him, her wide hazel eyes giving away nothing, then she sighed. "Fine."

"You have the most beautiful sigh. Is that particular one reserved just for me or do you use it all the time?"

"Now, Hudson, what kind of woman would I be if I just went around sighing at every man I came into contact with? Really. It's just when I'm around you."

"I'm touched."

He then tuned to check on the Kents. They weren't in

the best spot, so he called out to them, "Take five steps inland, please."

The ground over there was firmer and smoother beneath the snow. While he'd never lost a guest, never even had one seriously injured, he didn't want to risk it, especially in front of Nat. He had her recommendation on the line. Though, if he was honest with himself, something he was beginning to wish he avoided, he'd wanted to impress her.

"So earlier you said you were thinking of outing ideas?" she asked as they followed the Kents at a respectable distance to give them space. It seemed like they could be talking, and to his pleasure, they were still holding hands. It made him wish he was holding hands with Nat.

"Yeah, I was batting a few things around. I was thinking we could go down to Glens Falls for a day trip. Maybe we could set up some tickets for a show there or an afternoon at that winery."

"Both could be good," Nat said, flipping her notebook open again. "Dinner and a show to break up the outdoors stuff, plus, they could see each other all dressed up. That would certainly help in the romance department. The orchestra there is fantastic."

"You like the orchestra?"

"I was a part of the orchestra in school...well, at all my schools."

"That's a weird way to say, elementary, middle, and high."

"No, I literally mean *all* my schools." She slipped the notebook back into her pocket and kept her hands there. Her cheeks were pink with the cold, but her eyes sparkled as she talked. "We moved around a lot when I was a kid, since my dad was in the Air Force. There weren't a lot of constants in my life, but music is something that's universal."

"What do you play?"

"The violin."

"Were you any good?"

She smiled. "I haven't played in a few months, but I'm sure I could wow you."

"Sounds like you just offered me a private concert."

"No way," she said, the shake of her head making her ponytail bounce. The strands of red in her strawberry hair were more pronounced in the sunlight. "I don't really play for people, mostly myself."

It was strange to think he'd never really seen her out like this, so relaxed and free from her personal constraints. She'd never smiled so easily or given so many details of herself before. Hudson needed to figure out how to keep her in that moment of peace.

"Okay, so you're a musical genius. What other things are you ridiculously good at?"

"Come on, I don't want to brag."

"It's not bragging if I'm asking. Give me your stats."

She snorted. "My stats? What am I, a baseball card?"

"Were you interested in sports?" he asked.

"Not officially. I swam a lot, but never in a competitive setting. I really focused on the violin since the moving meant I couldn't exactly get a school sports career off the ground. How could I make a varsity team or get time on the field when I might have to leave in the middle of a season? It really wasn't worth it."

"You know, the picture you're painting of your childhood sounds pretty depressing."

"It wasn't!" she said quickly. "Did I hate having to move all the time? Of course. But I got to see and experience so many places and cultures. I speak five different languages I picked up along the way, and I have friends on four different continents... It was a wonderful way to grow up."

Her words weren't sharp, more like she was in a daze, flipping through her memories. In fact, the smile on her face didn't seem forced. It reached her eyes and with the sun behind her, the lake by her side, not a trace of make-up on her face, she was the most beautiful he'd ever seen her. He wanted to take a picture of it, to hold on to this moment for when she said or did something that drove him crazy. He just wanted to remember her like this with passion making her glow.

Hudson needed to backtrack before she clammed up again. "That sounds so exciting," he managed to say.

"It was. I'm all traveled out though, at least when it comes to living in new places. There are so many places I'd still like to see but I love the idea of having one spot to come home to once the trip is done."

He wanted to know more about this person he felt he didn't truly know at all. This new woman with friends everywhere, who played the violin and dreamed of seeing the rest of the world she hadn't as a kid. He had been pretty sure she'd never leave Lake George if she could help it, and each new layer she revealed was a surprise.

"Where did you live?" he asked. "Outside of the US I mean?"

"Germany, Spain, Japan, and Belgium."

"Wow. That's pretty awesome. I haven't really traveled much out of the US."

"Where are you from?"

"My family is from California, but I went to school in Colorado."

"Which college?" she asked eagerly. "One of my friends grew up on Peterson Air Force Base, so I've been to the state before."

Hudson wished he'd kept his mouth shut. This was going to be a downer. "Not college, military boarding school."

Her brows knit. "Really?"

"Really. From fourth grade to high school graduation."

"That's...that's..."

"Weird?" he offered in a tone he hoped kept things light. "I know. I don't exactly strike you as the boarding school kinda guy, but yeah, that's what my family did. Every generation went to some sort of boarding school. I just wasn't a fan of it." Hudson had to look away from her. All he saw in her gaze was confusion, like she was trying to figure him out, her eyebrows furrowed, her mouth open slightly like she'd be asking more questions. No, not on the schedule for today. That was quite enough about his past. "Hey, look, there's the path into the trees."

Nat

NAT WASN'T SURE how things had gone from lighthearted to heavy so fast. She was actually beginning to have a little fun talking to him, but to hear he'd grown up in a military boarding school and hated it made her heart clench. She appreciated and respected the military and felt it had actually made her a better person. Her brothers had followed in her dad's footsteps and were serving too. They loved the life. But at the same time, she also knew it wasn't for everyone. She had several friends growing up who despised the rules and regulation. She couldn't imagine how hard it would be to live that life for so long and to hate it.

Instead, she focused on the path ahead not the pity he clearly didn't want from her. Towering trees dusted in snow framed the faint path which had seemingly been untouched since the flurries. The way the evergreens and spruce trees were covered in powdery white made her think of Christmas and the taste of hot chocolate and the scent of cookies baking. They all glittered in the sunlight, shining like diamonds, and dripping with icicles.

The land around Lake George had always been a gorgeous wonderland. It was why people came from all around to spend time on its shores. But even after working there for so many years, knowing the lodge inside and out, Hudson had managed to take her breath away with one short walk through the trees. She couldn't believe all of this beauty had been right in her own backyard; she had just been so focused on other things and didn't realize the world around her.

"This is gorgeous," she said to Hudson. She'd lowered her voice as if the sound of it would make the snow fall from the branches, which in all reality probably wouldn't ruin the scene at all, just add to the magic.

"Isn't it? Summer is great by the lake, but you can't beat a scene like this in winter."

The Kents were still ahead, their voices rising as Hudson and Nat drew near. They seemed to be doing okay as far as she could tell. But for the next few moments, she allowed herself to forget about her mission and just live in the now. She sort of felt like a Victorian-era chaperone, trailing a courting pair of lovers as they took their weekly stroll.

When they stepped beneath the canopy made by the trees, they were surrounded by the sparkle of snow, walking on a bed of glittering pine needles. The world was quiet there, save for the voices of the Kents. Every so often the breeze would shift some branches, letting flakes fall from overhead. It was like being inside a living snow globe.

"You act like you've never been out here before," Hudson said with a laugh.

"Terry and I just started running outside. Before, I could only get her on the treadmill. Typically, I run near my apartment and…well it doesn't look anything like this."

Then she turned to Hudson, suddenly completely in awe of him. This idea, this path, it had been all him. Yet again he showed her he was more than capable, he was creative. "Hudson, I misjudged you. This is incredible. I can't imagine not falling in love looking at something like this."

"Falling back in love, right? Isn't that what you meant?" Hudson asked.

"Oh, obviously. Just look at them." She waved a hand at the Kents.

Marvin was taking some pictures of Mina, and she was smiling beside a large spruce tree. Nat focused her attention there and not on what she had just said. But out of the corner of her eye, she watched Hudson. He'd corrected her, clearly hearing that she'd said falling *in* love instead of falling *back* in love. What did he think about her weird choice of words? It seemed like some sort of slip, some strange thing that came out, beckoned by the magic of snowfall.

It made her feel foolish. It wasn't like she was in love with Hudson. She may have had real feelings for him, or at least she thought she did, but that was pretty much it. She only knew him at a surface level, as a coworker, and maybe now as a friend. But the L word was out of the question.

"Yeah, that looks better than eating dinner alone," Hudson murmured, stuffing his hands in his jacket pockets.

Mina and Marvin began walking again, and Nat and Hudson hung back to give them more privacy before Nat decided to follow at a distance. "Taking them outside today was a good call."

"Nothing like nature to bring you back to the simple things in life. It's why I suggested this. I genuinely thought it would help." Hudson followed behind her. She heard his footsteps, but he didn't say anything. She continued wandering down the path, her fingers brushing over the tips of snow-kissed branches.

"You seem to be enjoying yourself. Does that mean I'll get an excellent recommendation for California?" Hudson asked.

"I thought you didn't want it." She stopped walking and turned to face him. Their conversation earlier had annoyed her. She was trying to make things right with him, and he'd been dismissive and sarcastic. But in the woods—in his natural habitat—he was different. She couldn't figure him out and the attempts were making her head spin.

"No, the recommendation sounds great. I'd appreciate it."

She thought about saying thank you, or it was no trouble, or maybe even something quick-witted. But instead she didn't say anything. With Hudson standing close to her, birds chirping in the trees, and the Kents too far off to overhear them, her heartbeat suddenly felt too loud, too noticeable. She was swept up in the moment, in a snow globe of Hudson's making. She just had to hope, that for maybe a few more moments, Hudson wouldn't open his mouth and say something to ruin it.

And he didn't. Actually, he didn't say anything. He just reached out, tucking a stray stand of hair behind her ear, his bare fingers warm as they gently grazed her cheek. Her eyes closed, holding on to that tender sensation for an extra second. And then she heard Mr. Kent call out for Hudson.

They both jolted, as if struck by lightning, and strode up the path in search of their charges. Mr. Kent and Dr. Kent were no longer lovebirds taking pictures. Instead, Dr. Kent was leaning against a tree examining her nails and Mr. Kent was coming over to Hudson. Remembering his insistence that "guy code" needed to be respected, Nat decided to humor him and talk to Dr. Kent instead.

"Is everything alright?" Nat asked as Dr. Kent fixed her wind-tousled hair.

"Oh, it's fine. Marvin was just worried we were getting too far ahead."

"And the walk itself?"

She smiled softly. "It's cold, but I'm really enjoying myself. I can't remember the last time I took a good, long walk like this. It's so refreshing."

"That's great to hear. Is Marvin enjoying it as well?"

"I suppose. Is there a place to get coffee or something to warm up after this?"

"Of course. Have you been to the cafe yet?"

"No, is that the little place near the pool?"

She nodded, noting that Hudson and Mr. Kent were beginning to walk deeper down the forest path, and she went to follow them as she spoke to Dr. Kent. "They actually make fantastic Valentine's Day hot chocolate. Instead of regular milk chocolate, it's this special kind of pink cocoa and they top it with pastel marshmallows. When we get back, I can take you and Mr. Kent there for a cup to warm up. It also has a great view of the lake. Couples love it there since there's nothing but love seats this time of year."

"Is there anywhere at the lodge that doesn't have a great view of the lake?" she asked with a laugh.

"Not really, but it was built that way on purpose. It's hard to tell by looking at it from the ground, but the lodge is built like a crescent moon, with long wings to be able to see Lake George from nearly all the places it counts, like the restaurants and guest areas. Even most of the rooms face the lake. The ones that face the entrance are generally staff quarters, the kitchens, things like that."

"Was it always so big?"

Nat dove into her mental notes about the history of the lodge. "No, not always. The original Sutton family built the first section in what is now the lobby. In the beginning, it was sort of a waystation for fur traders and travelers in the 1800s. They had a small kitchen—which is now where the main fireplace is—a handful of rooms, and a small central area where people would eat. Over time, they began to add more rooms, build a bigger kitchen, and start cultivating the luxury you see today."

"And how long have you been here?"

"Thirteen years, if you can believe it."

"Oh my. Did you work here in high school?"

"No, I started working here right after I graduated, when my parents settled in Saratoga Springs." And that was when Nat realized, Dr. Kent was being evasive. She seemed to keep avoiding any question that had to do with her husband in favor of literally anything else, from drink options to Nat's career. She'd need to stay on her toes. "You know, my parents have been married for thirty-seven years and have never been here. How long have you and Mr. Kent been married?"

Dr. Kent scoffed. "Too long."

"I'm sorry?" Nat asked. She could feel the customer service smile she'd put on slipping off her face. She certainly didn't expect that sharp of an answer.

"Oh, don't worry about me. I just mean I've been with Marvin for a long time."

"Will you tell me about it?" It made Nat terribly uncomfortable to ask, but she felt she needed to connect with her like Hudson connected with Mr. Kent. She rarely pushed for information from guests like this. She believed it wasn't her business if they didn't want it to be, but she felt she had no choice.

"Oh, well, we met when I was just starting college. He worked at a little coffee shop I'd study at some nights, and I'd usually end up leaving when he did when the shop closed. You get to know a lot about a person that way. A year later we were engaged. A year after that, we got married and moved into a tiny apartment near campus while I got my degree, then moved again while I got my doctorate, then again…well, almost forty years and we both grew up."

"That has to be so romantic, though," Nat said, trying to inject warmth into her words. "Growing up with someone, being by them through all aspects of life…I'm pretty envious of you actually."

"You shouldn't be. I'm pretty jealous of you. Natalie, you have your whole life in front of you and so many options. I mean, if you wanted to fly to Paris, you could."

"But, Dr. Kent, you're retired. You could do it too."

"Marvin complained the whole flight here, and it wasn't that far from Texas. He's the kind of man to stay put when he can, and he planted his roots in St. Louis too long ago to get too far now. Louise is the only reason he even considered Texas. Trust me." She took a deep breath, still not looking at Nat. "Let's head back. I'm a little tired and could use a nap before dinner."

"Right, we can do that. I'll get Hudson." She jogged up

to Mr. Kent and Hudson and tried to smile. "How are you doing, Mr. Kent?"

"Great. This was quite the trip," he said jovially. He didn't come off as someone set in his ways, but it wasn't as if she truly knew him.

"Oh, it's not over yet." Hudson glanced around as if centering himself in the forest. "We just have a little farther to go."

"Dr. Kent is about ready to head back," she told him.

"Marvin, why don't you convince her to continue?" Hudson said. "It'll be worth it, I promise."

"I'll give it my best shot."

Nat watched him go. "Does it seem to you that he's trying a lot more than she is?" she asked Hudson quietly.

"Definitely."

"Well, I guess I'll ty to talk to her about that. She mentioned they've been together since she was eighteen, and I have a feeling that they grew up together, then apart."

"Marvin mentioned that too. Not to break guy code, but it seems to me they're both just a little lost without their jobs. Retirement isn't going well."

"That's good intel."

He grinned. "I'm going to take you out in nature more often. You like me better out here."

"Don't worry, we'll be back to the resort soon and I'll roll my eyes at you again."

"Thank goodness. I can't quite get through my day

without it."

As they got deeper into the wood, Hudson began to pick up the pace. Nat didn't see what the rush was, since she knew by checking his schedule that day that he wasn't due to be anywhere else. But he seemed enthused to reach their mystery destination.

Suddenly, he took a left off the path, stepping over a bare bush and holding his hand out to her. "Here, let me help you."

Nat moved to place her palm on his but instead he grabbed her around the waist and hoisted her over the bush to the other side. The motion was so unexpected, it took her a moment to realize what had happened. But soon she was stepping out of the way so Mr. Kent, then his wife, could join her on the other side.

To her surprise, they weren't on a path anymore. The trees were closer together, leaving no room for a pine needle lane. She sidled up to Hudson, and asked, "Where are we going? I thought we were supposed to turn around at the marker."

"Good things come to those who wait," he replied sagely.

"Waiting in the woods generally doesn't end well for people. On my schedule, I have—"

He plucked the notebook from her fingers and stuffed it

into his back pocket. "Live a little, Nat, and trust me."

Her fingers itched to snatch it back. "To be clear, this is a good surprise?"

"One of the best. I just found this place. This is the first time I've brought anyone with me."

"Should I be honored or worried you're going to kill me, and no one will find the body?"

"What kind of murderer do you think I am? It's on the staff schedule that we're together now. They'd know I did it. Really, Nat. I expected better. Plus, I'll never get that job in California if the Kents tell Sutton they witnessed me kill you. Come on, just trust me."

Nat hated surprises. She even liked to pick out her own Christmas and birthday gifts, so she'd never be caught off guard. But she would do what Hudson asked and hoped it wouldn't be anything too outlandish. However, everything Hudson did seemed to be big, so for all she knew, they could've been going to a pasture filled with unicorns.

They picked over the snowy underbrush. Nat was going to turn around and suggest the Kents hold hands through this trek but, much to her pleasure, they already were. Whatever had soured Dr. Kent's mood before was gone, replaced by that same lightness as earlier. Maybe she liked surprises.

Nat was so caught up in what they were doing, she stumbled over a pile of branches. Hudson caught her hand, stopping her from falling. As soon as she was righted, she expected him to let go, but he didn't. Through the soft knit of her gloves, his hand was impossibly warm. Hudson as a person was warm, both figuratively and literally. She wished she'd seen this side to him so much sooner. It would have saved her a lot of headaches and him a lot of lectures, and they could have done so many unforgettable things together for the guests. And maybe for her too.

Hudson had an easy way about him. He seemed to pull things out of people, even herself. She normally didn't tell others personal stories about herself. Dropping breadcrumbs like that was pretty pointless, at least when it came to those who would probably end up leaving her life at some point.

Having to cut ties or nurture friendships from afar was one of the hardest parts of being in a military family. Just when you became comfortable with someone, you were shipped off to a new base and had to start all over. Or worse, they were. It was like a candle being lit at both ends. Either you left, or they did. And Hudson was no different. He practically had a deadline ticking like a bomb, but she still didn't let go of his hand. Right now, on the secluded path, the only place he was going was with her.

"Here it is," Hudson told them, holding back the branches of an evergreen tree.

The Kents went first and Nat trailed behind, already missing the warmth of Hudson's hold on her.

She hadn't known what to expect from Hudson's side trip, but it wasn't what she saw in the clearing. In the center of a circle of trees was a well made of pale stones stacked waist high, an old iron arch looped above it, a hook where a rope or chain may have once been hanging from the center. But the rocks weren't exactly plain. There were designs etched into them, worn by time and sprinkled with snow.

"What is this?" Mr. Kent asked.

"This well belonged to an old homestead," Hudson explained, giving the stone a pat. "The house that used to sit just a few yards north is gone, but this remains."

Nat leaned over and looked down. It was too dark below to see if any water was left, but she assumed it would be ice if there was.

"What's it now, then? A wishing well?" Mr. Kent patted his pockets. "Too bad I don't have any change."

"Lucky for you, I have a quarter for each of you." Hudson pulled out a handful and passed one each to the Kents. "Remember to only wish for something you really want. Something really important."

"This is a great find," Nat whispered as the Kents went to the well.

"Thanks. It's not really all that interesting, but the story about wishes helps."

She nudged him with her shoulder. "You're so sly."

He held a coin up between his fingers. "It can't hurt to give it a try."

"Seriously?"

"Come on, Nat. Worst thing that happens is nothing

happens. Best case scenario, your wish comes true. So, go ahead, take a leap of faith."

Hudson

AS THEY HEADED back from the hike, Hudson was feeling pretty pleased with himself. The wishing well had worked out perfectly. Well, alright, he didn't know what the Kents had wished for, but it was the perfect backdrop for a romantic encounter. They'd taken some pictures there and they both seemed pleased.

He had watched Marvin, trying to look after his wife, to take her hand, to ease her over rocks. It had seemed sweet to him. True, it could've just been him being polite, but it was a start. Though, he wasn't spying on them as much as he should've. Nat kept getting in the way. And now, walking back, he had the urge to hold her hand again, not necessarily for safety either. He'd liked the way it felt. He'd actually taken off his glove to feel closer to her. As long as they were connected, he wasn't cold, and craved more of that same sensation.

Hudson knew she'd love the wishing well. In fact, she was probably considering creating a special little pamphlet for her box to describe it to guests. He figured pretty soon he'd be taking couple after couple up there so they could wish for endless happiness or some other cheesy romantic future together. But what mattered, at least at that moment, was that he'd taken Nat first. While the other couples didn't know, and he'd never tell them, it would always, in his mind, be their spot.

He shook that idea off for the moment as they walked back into the lodge, ready for her to become customer service robot, leaving fun and light Nat in the forest with the trees.

"I'm frozen to the bone," Mina said, still tucked deeply within her scarf.

"Dr. Kent, I could bring two cups of that hot chocolate for you and Mr. Kent to share in your room if you'd like," Nat offered as they walked into the lobby.

"No, no. He was telling me all about your lovely book collection in the study. I'm sure he'll be happy there. Besides, I could really go for a nap." Then she turned to Hudson and extended her hand out. "Thank you for the walk. It was cold, but worth it. And, Natalie, I know it's a bother, but I really would love some hot tea to warm up. Any chance room service could send it up?"

"Of course. I'll bring it up myself."

With a thank you, she left toward the elevator, leaving Nat and Hudson standing by the doors and Marvin watching from the display of pamphlets.

Hudson looked to Nat and gave her a slight jerk of his head. He wanted to get some alone time with Marvin to sort out why things had changed so suddenly. Luckily, Nat seemed to take the hint and nodded once before disappearing down the hall toward the kitchen.

"Marvin, why don't we go take a seat by the fire on the patio outside?" Hudson began, trying to keep his tone relaxed and upbeat. "They usually set up a hot cider station. We can grab a cup and hang out for a bit."

"Yeah, alright, let's do that."

Hudson led the way down the main hall—past the gift shop, cafe, and the main restaurant—and opened a single glass door that led to the patio. A large, open space, in the warmer months it was used for wedding receptions and parties, with plenty of room for tables and a dance floor, and an unobstructed view of the water. Now in the colder months, there were heat lamps warming clusters of outdoor seating, and a large firepit, that was always moved closer to the lake in the spring and summer.

One of Terry's staff members was just finishing setting up the silver cart containing dispensers for apple cider and a number of plain white mugs. Hudson and Marvin each collected a cup and took two of the empty seats that surrounded the fire. It was still early, too early for the usual evening crowd that often drifted out when the sun began to set, although the sky was already taking on an orange hue.

Hudson leaned back in his seat, the mug cradled between his hands. "So, Marvin, is Mina okay? She left pretty suddenly."

"I don't know, kid," he said with a sigh. He was staring

into the fire, not looking particularly distressed, just very tired. "I mean, I thought things were going okay. I was trying to take an interest like you suggested but it's just not that simple. Before we came here, we were talking with divorce attorneys."

Hudson knew from the beginning that things with Mina and Marvin were serious but hearing the word divorce straight from the horse's mouth gave the entire situation more gravity. He'd spent all of this time focusing on himself and what helping the Kents would do for him. He'd never considered that he could be doing a lot more harm than good. It was easy for him to sit there and tell Marvin things were going to be fine, but these were real people, real people he couldn't just make do what he wanted, or what he thought was right. He could build them the perfect vacation, and it might still not mean anything in the end. Hudson wanted to call Mr. Sutton up right then and bail.

"I still don't get why she went upstairs, and you guys didn't go get a drink at the cafe."

Marvin rubbed the back of his neck and shrugged. "I told her I didn't feel like getting hot chocolate. I thought after spending the whole morning and afternoon together, it would be okay for us to have some time apart, so I planned on going to the library."

"You told her you didn't want to spend time with her so you could read books?" Hudson wanted to shake him, or at least take away his library privileges for the remainder of his stay. He got that reading was fun and relaxing to a lot of people, but there was more on the line than him not reading the latest spy novel.

"When you say it out loud like that, it was pretty foolish of me. I really thought she would prefer it. She said she was tired."

"You don't need to get defensive, just try to see it the way she does. You went on this really cool walk together, she thought you guys would cozy up with some hot chocolate, maybe take a little nap before dinner, relax and enjoy each other's company, and you say you would rather read a book."

Marvin took a long drink of his cider. "I forgot how hard it was to date. Being married was easy, we were too busy to have to really work at it sometimes, you know what I mean?"

"Let's go back to when you first got together. What did you guys do when you were dating? Before you had your daughter and the real jobs?"

"Well, Mina loves to dance."

Hudson grinned. "Perfect, then I'll talk to Nat about your orchestra tickets. She and I had already discussed an outing that would incorporate music in a nearby town. First you'd go to a winery, then—"

Marvin placed a hand on his forearm. "Son, have you ever been to the orchestra?"

"Not a big one. Why, what's wrong?"

"It's a show. You're in your seat. Sure, she'd love to listen to the music, but it's not a get up and dance kind of thing. Besides, Mina loves to salsa."

Hudson tried to flip through all the amenities and lessons the lodge provided. Dance and music was an indoor thing, firmly in Nat's domain, so Hudson had never given it much thought. But this whole experience was about thinking outside the box, so he was sure they could figure something out.

"I bet Nat knows someone who could give you two a salsa lesson."

Marvin laughed lowly and stretched his legs out in front of him. "I can't tell you the last time I really got moving like that."

"Come on, I saw you on the outing today, you can handle some steps and dips. I'll go see Nat when we get inside and set something up."

"Speaking of Miss Natalie, when did the two of you start dating?"

Heat crept up Hudson's neck and settled in his cheeks. He choked down a bit more cider to give him a moment to collect himself. "No, uh, we're not dating. She definitely does not see me like that. We're totally just work...associates."

"She doesn't see you like that, eh? I wouldn't be so sure about that. I don't know, maybe I shouldn't be taking love advice from you when you're that clueless in your own life." And with that, Mr. Kent stood up. "I'm gonna go see a man about some more cider."

Hudson watched him go, stuck on his words. Maybe she just liked him in the fresh air because, in the office, she physically groaned when he came by. They'd never actually work, and he was already starting to get itchy about moving. That tended to happen once he was somewhere for more than a year. The towns and cities would feel too small, the faces around him too familiar.

He'd thought it might not happen at Hazel Oaks, since he was outdoors so much, breathing in the mountain air, but there it was, his urge to flee. No, not flee. Flee meant he was running from something. Hudson wasn't running. He was just moving on. Yeah, it was beginning to feel like it was time to move on.

Nat

TEA ON A tray, Nat headed up to Dr. Kent's room to make the delivery herself. She knocked on the door twice before Dr. Kent came to open it. She had red eyes and her mascara was smeared. Nat's heart fell to her stomach and as soon as the door was opened wide, Nat stepped in and put the tray on the coffee table.

"Dr. Kent, what's wrong?" She plucked a few tissues from the box beside the couch and handed them to her.

"Call me Mina, please." She dabbed at her eyes, but new tears kept falling, bringing more and more mascara with them.

"Come sit down," Nat said, leading her to the couch. She settled her on one side and sat on the other, bringing the box of tissues and placing them on the cushion between them. She wanted to pat Mina on the back or to do something to help her, but she didn't know what would be appropriate. Instead, she waited.

She waited through the tears and the sniffles until Mina finally took a ragged breath and then turned to face her. "Natalie, I know what you and Hudson are doing. I know why we're at this resort for Valentine's. I even see my husband trying some. But this…this is all fake, and as soon as we have a moment where there isn't an audience, it all falls apart. He wanted to read his book instead of sit outside and drink hot chocolate. When we go home, you and Hudson won't be there to make sure Marvin and I have fun or ensure he's attentive. Today…today was beautiful and I haven't spent that much time holding Marvin's hand in years but, it's all orchestrated. Hudson even told Marvin to take my hand in the first place. We're grown adults who are supposed to be in love. This isn't the way it should be."

Nat's heart rate began to race. Of course everything was planned. Surely they knew not every guest got the sort of treatment they did, or that things were just a little too done. But she hadn't thought that would hurt anything. Nat had just assumed they would appreciate the lengths to which one of their oldest friends, and even their own daughter, would go to see them happy together. The last thing she thought she would find in the room were tears.

"Isn't all love orchestrated somehow?" Nat asked. "We plan dates, get done up, celebrate things like anniversaries and Valentine's Day. Sure, Hudson told him to hold your hand but then Marvin didn't let go. Sometimes we all need a little help."

"No, it's more than that. I just…what happens when he and I are at home and the fantasy that this place creates disappears? The marriage can't be fixed in a day. I can't look at a man who has become more of a stranger than a partner and say, let's be together again."

Nat despised the sentiment in her words. She sounded so defeated, like she didn't have the slightest bit of fight left in her. But she couldn't let her give up so easily. "Why not? Why can't you? You're right, we won't be here when you get home, but the two of you will. And when you fell in love with him, wasn't it fast? They say when you know, you know. How did you know?"

Mina dabbed at her eyes again, the faintest of smiles spreading across her tear-stained face.

"When I brought him home to meet my family the first time and my father took me aside to say he wasn't worth it, I knew he was. I didn't care that I might get cut off, I only wanted him."

"Getting cut off seems pretty intense."

"It was. I told you he used to work at that little cafe near my college, right? While he worked hard for every penny he ever made from the time he was thirteen, I was born with a silver spoon. My father hoped that when I went off to school, I'd bring home some blue-blooded business major or at least someone else going into the medical field. He never thought I'd come home with somebody like Marvin." Her eyes glazed over again, and the ghost of the smile disappeared. "That passion and need to be with him just isn't there anymore. I don't know how to get it back."

Nat sat for a few moments, choosing her words. Having things laid out in such an open and raw way really made her appreciate both the power she had in the situation and the powerlessness she felt. She had no idea how difficult it would be to change the lives of two people she didn't know a thing about. She knew their food preferences and the amenities Mina liked at the spa, things she learned about all of her guests, but in reality, she had no idea how to fix things, because when it came down to it, only the Kents had that power.

"I think it's time for you to rebuild that passion," Nat began. "If we can just get a spark, we can nurture it here, and you can continue to build it when you're home. If you're always searching for more ways to be closer, you'll never lose that passion again."

"My worry is that we'll never find it."

"I understand that, but I guess if I were in your shoes, I wouldn't be so much afraid you'll never find it. I'd be more concerned what you're going to think six months from now, a year from now, ten years from now. Are you going to wish you'd at least tried this one last time?"

Mina took a deep breath. She wasn't crying, but she didn't exactly look happy. "I guess I have a lot to think about. Thank you, Natalie, and please, will you keep this conversation to yourself? I don't want Marvin or Hudson to know all of this."

"Of course. That is one thing you don't need to worry about. Please let me know if I can do anything else."

Nat went back down to the lobby feeling as though someone had deflated her balloon. She'd been selfish. She'd been worried she get fired if she couldn't get the Kents back together. And here was this very real woman in very real pain. Pain that Nat wasn't sure she could fix. Or really that she should fix. What did she actually know about love? She'd never experienced it herself. Not that real, all-consuming, explode if they're not there sort of love reserved for movies and novels. Mina and Marvin had that once. What was that saying? It was better to have loved and lost than never experienced it at all? She couldn't remember it exactly but she understood the notion. Mina wasn't the only one who had some thinking to do.

With these thoughts swirling in her mind, she didn't see Hudson until he was right on top of her in the hallway that led to her office, nearly knocking into him.

"Whoa there," he said, grabbing her arms. "You alright?"

Nat steadied herself physically, grateful she had her sneakers on and not her heels. But even though she was no longer a bodily risk to anyone around her, she still couldn't look Hudson in the eye. She didn't know how. How could she explain all of this to him? "Hey, I'm in my 30s and I don't think I've ever really found love and now I'm trying to help a couple in their 60s find love, despite the fact that I should probably be learning from them. I'm clearly out of my element and you were right to think I need help but, honestly, I don't think there is enough help for me, and I'd just really like to go run ten miles. Maybe physical exhaustion would stop my mind." Oh yeah, now that was attractive. So instead of unloading all of that onto him, Nat decided to keep it simple.

"Yeah, I'm fine. I talked to Mina, and I'm so sad for them."

"I know!" he said forcefully. "Man, I just want them to get back together. I know Marvin wants to, but he isn't sure how to win her back and he keeps sabotaging himself."

"Mina is worried once they leave here, things will go back to where they were: strangers roaming the same house. She thinks this bubble of the resort is going to pop."

Hudson took a step back, shoving his hands in his pockets and shrugging. "Alright, well we gotta get out of here. There's nothing more we can do tonight."

"Yeah, I'm gonna head home. Maybe go for a run."

"A run? We just did that hike."

"Yes, it's just exercise is how I think. It slows my mind down."

"Then let's go exercise."

Nat raised her eyebrows at him, folding her arms in front of her. "If you're about to tell me you want me to run some sort of crazy obstacle course, I'm going to have to pass. I've seen that on TV and I don't have time to recover from some crazy fall in the hospital."

"Hey," he said, hands up in front of his chest. "I'm just suggesting we do something like Topgolf. You know, get our aggression out by smashing the balls as far as they'll go. We can even get a little competition going to keep things fun."

"I've never swung a golf club in my life."

"Well then this will be fun. Let's go."

CHAPTER SIX

Hudson

HUDSON SAT IN his Jeep, waiting for Nat in the drive-way that looped around the front of the resort. She had to go get her purse and turn in the schedules for the next day. He'd told her to meet him out front so he could drive. She could have easily followed him in her car, but he couldn't stop his conversation with Marvin from swirling around in his mind every time he so much as looked at her. He needed to try and really figure out what was going on between them, or if anything at all was going on between them.

Grateful for the few moments alone to process, Hudson leaned his head against the steering wheel. He and Nat were going out. Well, maybe not *going out* but they were leaving the resort, they didn't have guests with them, it wasn't an assignment, and he did intend on paying. It was probably the closest thing he'd get to a date with her. Maybe. He thought about what Marvin had said again, how she seemed to like him.

That was certainly not the vibe Hudson got when he was around Nat. She rolled her eyes at him so much he almost wasn't sure what eye color she had. Alright, that was dramatic. She had hazel eyes. Bright hazel eyes that matched her strawberry hair perfectly. Eyes that, on their hike, had beamed up at him. Eyes that, looking back at him a few minutes ago, had broken his heart. She wasn't just worried about work; she genuinely cared about these people. The customer service robot had feelings. Seeing that crack in her armor, Hudson wanted nothing more than to fix it. He couldn't imagine her going home alone and just running mile after mile. Maybe it was his primal fixing instincts, maybe he was becoming a softie, or maybe it was because Nat was always taking care of others and, for whatever reason, Hudson needed to see her smile tonight. And he wanted to be the cause. But yeah, definitely no feelings.

The main lobby doors opened, just as Hudson looked up. Nat was speaking to one of the valets, the teen who worked nights and weekends as he saved up for his first semester at college. They were tucked away from the wind beside one of the stacked stone pillars that held up the *porte-cochère*. Normally a brilliant white, contrasting with the dark wood of the exterior, everything seemed to glow orange and red between the stones and the dusting of snow that hadn't melted, despite the sun of the day.

Hudson remembered the first time he'd come to Hazel Oaks. It had been in the heat of summer when everything around the lodge was green with life. When you were outside, it was hard to distinguish between the chattering of the guests and the singing of the cicadas. He'd taken in the large windows and the specific scent of fresh water that only came beside a lake the size of Lake George. He'd fallen in love with it at once, even though he'd already been telling himself he'd only be there for a year or two, tops. Maybe he had more in common with Marvin than he thought.

He was still staring when Nat turned and saw his car. She gave him a small wave and then said something to the valet before jogging toward him. He hopped out to open the door for her.

"Thanks," she said softly before climbing into the Jeep.

Hudson closed the door and walked around to the driver's side. As he pulled out of the circle and drove through the path of trees to get to the main road, he and Nat sat in uncomfortable silence. He wasn't the "hold your hand and listen to your feelings" type of guy. Probably because he didn't have many long-term relationships. He much preferred to keep things light. It was one of the reasons he'd suggested Topgolf. He needed to take control of the situation.

"So, you've never swung a golf club?" he asked as he followed the familiar roads to the more metropolitan area.

"No, it just never came up."

"Well, I happen to have an excellent golf swing, so I'll either be of great help or you'll be dutifully impressed.

Possibly both."

"Oh yeah?" Nat asked, finally smiling. Well, maybe smirking was a better description. "Is that why you suggested this? You wanted to impress me?"

"What guy doesn't want to impress a pretty girl?" He turned to look at her and gave her a full-toothed cheeky grin.

"Nice line, does that work with all your dates?"

His stomach did a flip. Did she think it was a date? "Usually."

Nat laughed. "Why did I think this was going to be a good idea?"

"Because I'm charming, mildly entertaining, and honestly, you needed a break. This whole thing with the Kents was getting a little heavy. At least, I know it was for me."

"It was for me too. I guess for the first time I realized I could truly ruin a marriage. I'm starting to wish I'd never agreed to this. It's too much pressure."

"As if you had a choice. Mr. Sutton wasn't exactly subtle about any of this. And the two of them are so lost, I don't think you could do any more harm. Really, you care so much, and you have this big heart. Anything you do will be well placed. If someone tries to say different, let me know, I'll lose them in the woods."

She laughed again. He glanced at her briefly as they hit a red light, hoping to see those hazel eyes looking back at him, her real smile glowing in the fading sunlight. Instead, he saw her wipe a tear. He'd cracked the robot.

"Don't go getting all sweet on me, Hudson. I won't recognize you."

"Not a chance, Nat. Not a chance."

TOPGOLF WAS PRETTY crowded for a Sunday night with nearly every bay full. After a short wait, they went to their own section and ordered sodas, mozzarella sticks, nachos, and a sampler platter of fried food that would make the health-conscious coaches at the gym give him a stern lecture.

Their bay was the last one on the second floor, and they sat close together on a sleek black couch with the food and drinks spread before them on a low table, and heaters blowing from behind them. Top 40 pop music was playing overhead, and the constant thwacks of clubs and cheers of the other players gave the whole place a cheerful mood Hudson had desperately needed.

They were alone for the first time ever outside of the lodge. There were dozens of other people around, players, waitresses, spectators, but being holed up in the corner, away from Hazel Oaks added an intimacy to their evening. It made Hudson nervous to have nothing to distract them. Still, he wished he thought of taking her somewhere like this before, away from the lodge and the guests to really get to know each other. Maybe they wouldn't have spent so much time fighting if they had.

They had ordered their food as soon as they had got to their place, and it had just arrived when Hudson had finished setting up the first game on the little touch screen. He'd explained they were going for distance and put their names in. He thought just letting her hit the ball as hard as she could would let her loosen up and keep the game interesting. She seemed the type to have beginner's luck. More than that though, part of the reason they were here was to get out some of their frustrations and anxiety regarding the Kents. What better way to do that than to hit the ball as hard as you can?

"You ready for this?" Hudson asked as he picked up a mozzarella stick from the basket and went to look at the display of men's clubs.

Nat sat back in her seat and regarded him over the top of her soda cup. "No pressure, but I will be judging your first shot harshly."

"Wow, I wasn't prepared for that comment."

"It's like with the Olympics. I'm going to watch you a couple times, maybe max five times, and I'll be an expert commentator who can't actually do the skill myself."

"Well, at least you're aware." He finished his food and selected a driver, giving it a few exploratory swings. "You know this computer is actually going to judge the distance. When you hit the ball, it goes to a net with a sensor that will give you the distance, and then a score. You don't actually have to critique me. The computer will do it."

"That takes the fun out of it."

"In that case, I look forward to your judgment."

He looked down at the ball, adjusted his grip, settled his feet, and swung. The ball went far but missed the two-hundred-foot target he'd been aiming for. Hudson turned around and glanced to Nat. "I'm waiting for my score."

"No, I can't score yet. I have to see a couple different swings and whatever. You know, variety. I don't even know what you're doing or aiming for."

"Basically, you aim for whatever you think you can hit. The balls used in Topgolf are different than regular golf balls. They lack the same heft that let real golf balls go the distance." He put another ball on the tee. "So, what's going to happen is I'm going to go for that two-hundred-foot marker. I get ten turns, and then you get ten turns. At the end it'll give us our final scores." He adjusted his stance and the grip on the club and swung again.

Nat clapped.

"What's with the fanfare?"

She popped a chip into her mouth. "Isn't that what people do when they watch golf? Clap politely after each hit?"

"I mean you're not wrong, but it wasn't that great of a drive."

Hudson finished his round with Nat clapping politely after each swing, sometimes calling out a random number, her favorite being forty-two. When it was her turn, she seemed less than enthused as she looked over the women's clubs. Now it was his time to shine.

"You ready to wow me?" he asked, taking a sip of his soda.

"I would be if I knew what I was doing." She stood up and wandered over to the clubs. "They all look so different. Does it matter which I pick?"

He followed her over and pointed to each selection. "Here, you have hybrids, drivers, and irons. For now, I'd go with a hybrid." He picked one for her and she took it, looking unsure. "Alright, let's see what you've got."

"What?"

"Yup, your turn. Go on."

"You aren't going to show me?"

"I need to see what you've got first, then I'll critique your swing."

Nat sighed and rolled her eyes, a smile spreading on her face. "Oh great one, I don't even know how to hold this. A little help please?"

"Since you referred to me as my given name, yes." He gently took her hand and pulled her to the front of the bay. He positioned her correctly, telling her to bend her knees a bit, and then stood behind her, his hands on her shoulders. "Okay," he said in her ear. "Do you see all those brightly colored circles on the green? Those are targets. You want your ball to fall around the ones with the highest points. Each target has a number next to it; that tells you how much it's worth. And there are targets everywhere so you'll get points, no worries there."

"That's not my worry right now."

"What is?"

She turned around and faced him, the eye contact almost too intense. On the one hand, he was desperate to look away, but on the other, he wasn't sure if he could. "If I told you, I'd have to kill you." She patted his chest, her hand resting there for a few moments. Hudson knew she could probably feel his heart trying to burst through his shirt at just her touch. He smiled wryly, pleased nonetheless. Then, she dropped her hand, turned from him, and got back into her golf stance. He reached down and adjusted her grip, his fingers lingering on her hands just a moment too long. "Alright," he said softly behind her. "Give it a strong swing. I'll be watching."

He went back to his seat and watched her try to swing. The club scuffed the floor before even reaching the ball. She took a few steps back and tried it again, but again scuffed the floor. She sighed loudly and tuned to look at Hudson.

"Yes?" he asked, tilting his head to the side.

"What am I doing wrong?"

"There's quite a list."

"Care to share?"

Hudson shrugged his shoulders and took another sip of soda. He thought standing next to her in front of the tee was where he wanted to be, but watching her now, he wasn't sure he wanted to get up. She'd taken off her jacket ages ago and was left in her leggings and a pale green sweater that brought out the forest-colored flecks in her eyes. The wind was blowing slightly sending her hair haphazardly around her. And while all of that seemed like enough of a distraction, it was the scowl on her face that amused him the most. She needed his help, and he needed to make her smile again. But he wanted to play with her a little bit, the sassy woman certainly gave him enough of a hard time.

"If I do, I'd have to kill you. Did I say that right?"

"Nicely played." Nat tried again and still wasn't able to hit the ball. She turned to him, putting one hand on her hip, pursing her lips. "I'm thinking you're a bad teacher."

He waited a second before responding, stroking his chin with his hand as if he was considering letting her continue making a fool of herself. "Whoa, don't question my skills. Let's start with going over the grip again," he said, moving to stand next to her, hoping explaining things would keep his mind from wandering to other possible nights out together, cozy evenings by the fire at the lodge and dates, real dates, far away from Hazel Oaks where she could really turn off her customer service self and be simply Nat. "First, you need to fix your grip. Interlock your left pointer finger with right pinky finger, like this." He mimicked the hold for her and watched as she copied, her brow knit in concentration. "Now make a V shape with the thumb and pointer finger of your right hand, then close your fingers."

"Like this?"

"Exactly."

She stood there frozen, staring at him. "Now what?"

"Put your feet shoulder-width apart, then swing."

Nat did as he asked and swung. The ball didn't go too far, and she frowned up at him. "Did I miss something?"

"Besides the target?" he teased as he set out another ball. "You just need to bring the club back farther and follow through. Oh, and try to not close your eyes. How can you hit a target you can't see?"

Nat looked at the ball, the green, and back to Hudson. "Do you think you can show me? I think I need your help doing the actual swing."

Hudson grinned. "Absolutely."

Nat

HUDSON CAME UP behind her, his hands over hers on the club, his arms draped over hers, his chest against her back. His woodsy scent of fire smoke and evergreen surrounded them, and she gripped the hybrid a little tighter, suddenly afraid her focus would shift from the club to him. They had never been so close to one another. It was both electrifying and completely foreign to her.

She hadn't thought he would put his arms around her when she asked for his help initially, but, in retrospect, she had seen this sort of move in enough movies and shows to know what she had been asking for here. Usually, the guys on television used this sort of move on the girls they were sweet on. Maybe this was just how he did it with everyone? On the other hand, it felt intimate. She wanted it to be unique.

"Earth to Nat," Hudson said in her ear with his usual cheery voice. "Are you listening?"

Nat blinked. She hadn't even realized he'd been speaking; her mind was too busy whirling. "Sorry, I was just thinking about something for another guest."

He gave her hands a small squeeze. "Remember, customer service Natalie isn't here right now. We're not working, you and I. There's no one you can help here. So, let's see how far you can hit this ball. I'm going to help you bring your arms back far enough and show you the follow through. Then I'll step back and you can swing on your own."

She nodded, a little disappointed he'd be letting go.

The sudden movement of swinging the club shocked her. He wanted her to really bring that thing around.

"Alright, go for it. I'm backing up now," he said in her ear, his cheek leaning against her head. She closed her eyes for a second, enjoying the closeness so much it shocked her more than swinging the club had.

Nat closed her eyes, trying to gather some semblance of mental fortitude and remember the tips Hudson had given her. She took a deep breath and swung. The ball hit one of the targets, and she cheered.

"Nice shot," he said, looking down at the screen. "That was a really good hit for someone who claims to not know how to golf. Did you just swindle me?"

"Never can tell."

"I'll just sit back here in case your beginner's luck wears out and you let go of the club or something in the back-swing." He grinned and went back to the couch, picking up his cup and taking a drink.

Nat set up another ball, adjusted her grip the way Hudson had shown her, then swung as hard as she could. She didn't hit a target, but it did feel really good. She could see why places like this were so popular. With each hit, and the satisfying smack of the ball on iron, she felt her tension melt away a little bit more.

Maybe it was time she and Terry spiced up their nightly exercise routine. She looked at Hudson, his face gleaming with pride for her. Then again, she thought, having Hudson as her golfing partner seemed like a bit more fun.

AS THEY HEADED back to Hudson's Jeep nearly two hours later, Nat was feeling completely energized. That could've had something to do with the memory of Hudson's arms around hers, the warmth of his hands sending jitters through her body, but she didn't want to think too hard about what that could mean. She just wanted to turn her brain off and bask in the memory of the feeling.

Hudson held the passenger door of the Jeep open for her like he did when he picked her up. She climbed in and put her seat belt on, and Hudson walked around the car and then got into the driver's side. He put the key in the ignition and then turned to her.

"Oh, I forgot to tell you. Marvin said that Mina used to love dancing. Like, salsa dancing, way back before they started a family and got caught up in their careers."

"Salsa dancing, okay. I can set that up. It was on my list of potential activities so I've done a bit of research." She reached into her purse for her notebook and flicked it open as Hudson put the car into drive. Then he reached up and flicked the overhead light on for her. "Thank you. Maybe we can turn the study into a little salsa club. There are already speakers for that light elevator type music that plays in there. I don't know, it could be intimate and special for them."

"I think that sounds great."

Nat's brain started going into overdrive. The lights in the study dimmed, so they could do some mood lighting. They could pick up some big bouquets of long-stemmed roses to put in various places. She could take Mina out shopping for a dress to impress Marvin. That whole idea of picking out an outfit with a man in mind was exciting. She pulled her phone out of her purse and began looking up dance instructors she could hire to come to the resort.

Suddenly the Jeep stopped, and Nat looked up. They were back at the resort. Hudson had parked next to her car in the employee lot. She turned to him, shoving her notebook and pen in her bag. Then she turned the light off. There was something a bit too much about it being on; she could see his features a little too perfectly. This just seemed like a moonlight kind of moment. "Thank you for tonight. It was really great and I needed it."

"Chalk it up to another one of my good ideas. Be careful, I think I'm ahead of you."

"Whoa, you're ahead? Tonight doesn't count."

"Why doesn't tonight count? I thought I was proving how guys are way more romantic. Wouldn't you consider tonight romantic?"

Nat didn't say anything at first. She wasn't exactly sure how she was supposed to respond. Why had he taken her out? She thought, at the time, it was him showing his feelings, those feelings Terry said were there. But with that comment she was no longer sure. Was he just trying to show her up? Still?

She felt like she couldn't trust her feelings or her instincts when she was around him. Like she'd thought before, it was hard to tell when he was serious or just joking. It had been a long day emotionally, physically, mentally, all of the allys. The heightened sense of awareness and focus that had come with playing golf was leaving her and her brain was becoming mush.

"I guess, if you're into that sort of thing," she said lightly before hopping out of the Jeep, hoping to leave him a little dazed and confused too.

Then Nat hurried into her car, waving at him before pulling out of the lot. Once she was out of his sight, she groaned. Her mind was a mess and she didn't know what to think. So, instead of focusing on the man with one foot on a plane to California, she focused on salsa.

CHAPTER SEVEN

Nat

NAT WAS AT the resort bright and early the next morning with a shiny, new to-do list. She wanted to talk to Mina and start setting up the salsa room so she could get the romance back on track. She'd emailed a couple instructors the night before and one had gotten back to her. They were all set for seven o'clock. While she didn't think it would happen so quickly, there wasn't a lot of availability for the instructor in the days leading up to Valentine's Day, so she would take whatever she could.

Now, to break the news to the couple.

Instead of putting the class on a schedule, she thought it would be much more romantic to have Marvin invite her. She pictured him writing her a lovely note asking her to join him for the evening. In order to orchestrate that, she thought it was best to have a meeting with Hudson. He had said he wouldn't be at the resort for another hour. So, with the patience of a gnat, she sat in her office, creating a shopping list to best transform the study.

She was running through it one last time when her landline rang. Before answering, she thought of chocolate, garlic bread, and stargazer lilies. She'd read in a book that if you thought of something that made you smile before you answered the phone, it would sound like you were smiling to the person on the other line.

"This is Natalie Keller, head concierge at the Hazel Oaks Resort, how may I assist you today?"

"Miss Keller, it's George Sutton here. How are you doing this fine morning?"

Nat instantly sat up straighter as if he could actually see her in the office. "I'm doing just fine Mr. Sutton. And yourself?"

"Well, I can hear that pep in your voice, Miss Keller, so I'm already doing better."

"Terry mixed up a new blend of coffee, and it's really getting me energized for the day."

"Ah yes, I always start my day with at least two cups, but if the blend at Hazel Oaks is as good as you say, I'll have to get a bag or two."

"I can certainly sort that out for you if you'd like?"

"Yes, please do. Anyway, I'm glad to hear you're well. Now, tell me, how are the Kents doing?"

Nat wasn't sure how to answer. On the one hand, he really did care and he seemed genuinely concerned about their happiness. On the other, it was really none of his business about their marriage. True, it was technically none of hers.

Oh, this whole thing was such a mess. She figured she'd mention what activities they were doing and not necessarily the emotions or the fragile state the marriage actually seemed to be in.

"They're all set up for private salsa lessons tonight, and they went on a nature walk yesterday. Sir, did you know there was a wishing well about three miles from the resort? It's this old stone setup and just truly amazing."

"I was wondering where they got to. I saw it once decades ago as a kid but could never seem to find it again. I'll have to go and check it out the next time I'm in town. I'm sure Ellie would love to see that."

"Yes, I'm sure she would," Nat said as if she knew his wife, when in reality they'd only met once at a Christmas party. But she could presume it would be a lovely walk for them. "Hudson found it, sir. He's really becoming an asset to the place."

"Good, I'm glad to hear he's pulling his weight and helping you out. Is there anything I could do to assist you? I already set up my secretary to put a little extra in the budget for outings and such, not just for my friends, but all the guests for Valentine's Day."

Nat made a note. "Thank you, sir. I'm sure we'll put it to good use. And I don't believe we need your help with anything just yet."

"That's what I like to hear. Well, I have another call in a few minutes, but I just wanted to check in."

"Absolutely, sir."

"Remember, call if you need anything but it sounds like you two are doing a great job."

"Thank you very much, Mr. Sutton."

"And, Miss Keller," he started softer and significantly calmer than his usual boisterous tone. "Thank you for doing this. Those people are family to me."

"Of course. They seem like genuinely good people."

"They really are." And without more of a goodbye, Mr. Sutton disconnected the line.

Nat leaned back in her chair, suddenly aware she was still sitting ramrod straight. She sighed heavily and closed her eyes. Mr. Sutton had so much faith in her to fix this relationship. She just wished she had the same amount. Maybe she could find a marriage counselor or someone in the area who had actual knowledge. Maybe she'd have some pointers or suggestions. Or maybe even a matchmaker to revive that first-date spark. Then, maybe once they were done with the Kents, the matchmaker could work her magic on Nat.

Hudson popped into her mind. How could he not? He'd been right; last night had been romantic. When he held onto her shoulders and spoke in her ear, or repositioned her hands on the club, all of those little things had felt good and right. And it made her wonder, how many other girls did he teach like that? That swagger didn't just appear overnight. He'd been gorgeous, probably since birth, and he'd been an activity instructor all over the country. And those activities left him fit. Fit enough to get any woman's attention. Did he have a girl in all the cities he's lived in that he'd take walking on tree-lined paths and out for dates?

To tell the truth, she didn't know if he was a player since they'd never discussed their private lives. And, at least to her knowledge, he wasn't dating anyone at work. He could've been a monk who swore off women before they met. But he was leaving for California. Sure, maybe not officially, but she certainly didn't want to pine for a man across the country. Goodbye was her least favorite word.

As if his ears were ringing, Hudson strolled into her office, a whole twenty minutes early.

"Well, well, well, you're early, Mr. Dougal. If I didn't know better, I'd think you were trying to suck up to me."

"Miss Keller, if I had any idea what would make you happy, I'd do it."

She frowned at this, then tilted her head to the side, a bit confused. "If I had any idea what that meant, I might have an answer." What kind of comment was that? She wasn't a difficult person. True, she was a little precise and she liked things orderly, but she wasn't a grouch.

"Don't worry about it. Anyway, I'm here. What can I do for you?"

"I have a salsa instructor coming at seven tonight. I've talked to Terry, and she's going to make them a late-night Cuban feast to go with the salsa theme. I don't actually understand what she's doing, but she's excited about it.

Anyway, I haven't told the Kents yet, and I thought you could talk Marvin into writing Mina a letter inviting her to dance."

"Why doesn't he just ask her? In person, like, get down on one knee, take her hand type stuff."

"No, that's a terrible idea. If he's not proposing a second wedding or giving her a new engagement ring type thing, he should definitely not get down on one knee. I don't know. Handwritten notes are just so personal, and people don't send them anymore. I just feel like it'll add an air of romance if I take her to the spa and she gets her hair done and then at the spa, a note is delivered by one of the junior concierges asking her to dance. Is that…you think that's ridiculous, don't you?"

He shook his head. "No, actually, I think it's the perfect amount of drama. Maybe I can talk to him about leaving her other notes too. That's something he could continue at home, outside of this bubble. That was something Mina was worried about, right?"

"Oh my gosh, that's brilliant!" She wrote a new note in her little book. "Yes, okay, I'll call the room and tell her about her hair appointment. You do something to get Mr. Kent to write the note."

"No problem. I can talk to him before my team meeting."

"What team meeting?" Nat couldn't remember seeing a meeting ever on his schedule.

"I like to get the team together every Monday to flesh out any issues and go over the weather forecasts. We usually do it outside so I guess you just haven't seen it."

"Of course. That meeting, right." She loved the sound of that. It was the kind of thing she'd do. In fact, she was surprised she'd never thought of it.

"Don't worry, Nat. I got this." And then he turned and walked out of her office.

Nat felt his absence more than she wanted to. Those feelings she'd barely admitted to Terry, the ones she wasn't even sure she had, they were seeming stunningly real. But instead of dwelling on it, since she couldn't do anything with them right now anyway, she got up and went to the study. She needed to figure out exactly how many roses to order from the florist.

Hudson

HUDSON HAD SEEN a side of Nat he didn't think she had, both in the woods and on their brief night on the town. The relaxed Nat who knew how to have fun and take a joke seemed to just be a fleeting part of what made Natalie Keller, Natalie Keller. Sitting across from her in her office, Hudson hardly could believe that girl was real. And then she'd smile at him, not her customer service smile, her real one, and he'd see that glimpse.

When he'd seen her sitting behind the desk with a tight bun and the pressed suit, part of him had been a little thrown off. He had half expected her to be there in a cozy sweater with her hair in a ponytail, or even better, loose around her shoulders. Of course, that was unrealistic, since she was back to doing her usual job, but it was just another reminder that their day together had been nothing more than a sliver of time, and now it was over.

He also wished he was brave enough to bring up last night. But this was work; he couldn't. Blurring those lines was something she'd certainly disapprove of. And that brought on the awkward. How was he supposed to act? And when you added that she was speaking to him without the warmth and sassy comments he was beginning to really enjoy, he almost wondered if he'd dreamed it.

Of course, he didn't have time to talk about it even if he'd wanted to. He had to work. Hudson hit the up elevator button in the lobby to go knock on Mr. Kent's door to see if he wanted to have breakfast together when he heard Nat calling him. He wasn't sure if they could be casual and light, or if she would expect him to act completely professional. He assumed since they were in the lobby, and in view of the guests milling around, he had to be professional. Those were the rules when she was in fancy clothes.

He turned around. "Yes, Natalie?" Maybe he'd use her full name at work and call her Nat outside. It might help him keep the distance.

She stopped for a second and frowned. Maybe she'd noticed he had called her by her full name. "Oh, um, I grabbed this cardstock from our supplies, and these felt markers. I thought it'd make a more romantic-looking note than the lodge stationary in the desk in the room. And here's an envelope so he can address it to her, and well, also because the valets are nosy."

"Can't have them reading the letter, can we?"

"No, we can't." She handed him the supplies and their hands touched.

Really it was just two of his fingers meeting with two of hers. All the same, it made him think of the nature walk and helping her swing a club. It made him eager to try and see her outside of work again. To confirm for himself that it wasn't just a dream.

"Is there anything else?" he asked her, suddenly desperate to get away before he said or did anything to let her know what he was thinking in this lobby. The name wouldn't help. He couldn't distance from the fact that he wanted to hold her in his arms.

"No, Hudson. I think that's everything." But she looked like she wanted to say something else. In fact, she opened her mouth, then shut it quickly. Finally, she looked around the lobby and nodded at one of the bellhops who was pushing an empty luggage cart toward her. "Sorry, I'm needed." And then she really was gone.

Trying to push all of the nonsense with Nat aside, he went up to the Lake View Suite. As he was walking down the hall, he saw Mina looking relaxed in a casual pink leisure suit. Hudson quickly did the best he could to put the supplies behind his back so she wouldn't see.

"Good morning, Dr. Kent, how are you doing?"

"Hello, Hudson. Please, call me Mina," she cooed in a singsong voice he'd never heard from her. "And I'm doing beautifully, thank you for asking. I'm just on my way to have my hair done. There's nothing like a trip to the spa to really boost your spirit."

"I'll take your word for it, ma'am. I pay twenty bucks to a barber and kinda hope it works out alright."

She laughed and went into the elevator.

Hudson continued down the hall and knocked on the Kent's door. He was hoping that since Mina was in such a good mood, Marvin would be too.

"Hey there, son, what are you doing here?" he asked when he came to the door.

"I'm on Operation Valentine business. I've got a plan for tonight and we need to go over it."

"In that case, you better come on in."

Hudson went to sit on the couch and spread the supplies on the coffee table. Marvin sat in one of the armchairs and listened as he explained about the private salsa lesson and the note idea. "You see, you could start now and continue it at home. Just little notes. 'Your perfume smelled lovely today,' or 'that color brings out your eyes,' little things to make her feel good and wooed and all that good stuff."

"I like it. And that woman knows my handwriting, so it'll mean something that I wrote them. Let's see..." He picked up one of the creamy cards, then put it right back down on the small pile. "Actually, I think I'll start on the pad the resort provided for the room. I'd hate to waste the good paper coming up with an idea." Marvin disappeared into the bedroom for a moment and returned with a note-pad. Then he sat back down, pulled out his glasses from his front pocket, and looked at the blank paper. He scribbled a few things down, crossing words out, and mumbling to himself.

Hudson felt a little awkward, sitting silently in the room. What was he supposed to do? Marvin didn't appear to want any help, and Hudson didn't want to offer it. The notes would mean more if they were authentically Marvin, using his phrases and his terminology. The last thing they needed was for Mina to think they were trying to pull one over on her.

Instead, Hudson read the news on his phone and got the latest updates on the Spartan Gym in California from his friends. Finally, about twenty minutes later, Marvin was satisfied. He signed the good paper, put it in the envelope, then handed it to Hudson.

"Do you want a piece? Maybe leave it for Natalie?" Marvin asked with a sly grin. He slid a piece across the table to him.

Hudson laughed loudly. This man had no idea. "We work together, sir. Trust me, I don't think she'd appreciate something like that."

"I'm just saying, you won't stay young long. Better find yourself a good woman before she finds herself a more courageous man."

"Hey there, Marvin, are you calling me a coward?"

"Son, I'm on the verge of divorce and before you, I was willing to just let it happen. Trust me, it takes one to know one."

"No, it's nothing like that. We went out to this sort of putting range last night. I thought it was great, you know, teaching her to swing a golf club and all that. And then, I saw her this morning at work and it was like last night never happened. She was all business. I'm not really sure how to do this whole dating a coworker thing. Frankly, it sounds like a bad idea."

"Hey, you're young. It's your choice, but if I were you, I wouldn't wait. Women like that usually have a line of men ready to do whatever it takes to win them over." Marvin stood up, then dropped one of the thin-tipped markers atop the paper. "Now, if you'll excuse me, you're going to have me shake and twist things that haven't moved in thirty years. I have some stretching to do and maybe some cardio. I should've told you we liked to nap."

Hudson nodded and rose from his seat. He left the unused cardstock and markers so he could write Mina another note and left Marvin to his miniature workout. He wanted Marvin to be right, but he still wondered if she'd ever date a coworker. He'd never seriously dated one since he was always moving. If he were honest with himself, he didn't really date seriously. And Nat, she didn't seem like the casual dater. That opened up a whole other set of concerns for him. Just another thing they didn't have in common.

As he stepped into the elevator, he thought about the cardstock paper he'd left with Marvin. He'd never written anything remotely close to a letter like the one Marvin had pushed him to write. He wouldn't exactly call it a love letter; he didn't even know what he might write, but he did know that it wasn't going to happen. He already felt a little on edge; the last thing he wanted to do was to put his feelings into words and have them physically there for all eternity. He had never been much of a gambling man, and this didn't seem like the sort of risk he wanted to take.

The hallway through the staff offices was empty, with most doors being closed. He walked a little slower when he reached Nat's. He told himself it was because he wanted to tell her Marvin was on board, but he knew the truth. He wanted to see if he could read her feelings on her features. He wanted to see if she would smile up at him in the same way she had in the forest. Or if she would give him the customer service special. He felt like that moment would be very telling.

Her office was empty. Hudson kept walking, pretending he wasn't bothered by her absence. He needed to get his act together.

Nat

NAT SIFTED THROUGH one of the racks of the charming boutique she and Mina had been in for the last half hour. Mina had just finished getting her nails painted when one of the concierges came into the spa bearing a letter on a silver tea tray with a single, long-stemmed red rose. Nat appreciated the attention to detail and gave Rebecca a grateful nod.

Once Mina had rendered the note, her eyes getting misty and she'd immediately begun to fret. She had all sorts of worries; not having a nice dress, the right shoes, and rusty dance skills. But none of those meant anything to Nat. As soon as she was done being primped and polished, Nat had hustled her into one of the lodge's cars for official business and drove her into town.

"How about this pink one?" Nat asked, holding up a dress with white polka dots.

"I'm not one for patterns," Mina said thoughtfully. "Maybe something black. When we used to go dancing all the time, I would always where this one gorgeous black number that hit just above the knees and swirled in the most immaculate way. It had this red sash and, wow, I kept that dress for years hoping we'd go out again. Actually, it may still be in my closet."

"Black it is then." She began looking for anything that resembled Mina's outfit. She wanted her to look beautiful, flirty, fun, and just have a spectacular evening. More than that though, she wanted to bring back that special feeling Mina used to have.

Soon the pair had gathered up a handful of dresses for Mina to try on. Nat sat on a low settee beside the dressing room, listening to Mina critique herself in the mirror. So far, the dresses had either been too short, too long, too tight, too plain, or too flashy.

"What about you?" Mina asked as Nat passed her a new dress over the top of the dressing room door.

"What about me?"

"Are you going to try anything on?"

Nat looked around the store. It was full of charming things, flowy skirts, beaded jewelry, dresses with fringed hems, and a wall of shoes made for dancing. "I don't know if any of these things are appropriate for work."

"Who said anything about work? You're young, you're pretty, don't you need a thing or two for nights out with your friends? Maybe even a date?"

"I don't think so…" Her mind immediately went to Hudson. They'd gone to Topgolf the night before, but next time they could go dancing or maybe go to the orchestra, out to dinner, somewhere candlelit and quiet. If there was a next time that is. She wanted there to be one, but she also wasn't exactly sure how to get that through to him at work. When he'd come into her office, she had to be professional, but she couldn't help her thoughts. Thoughts about how handsome he'd look over a candlelit dinner in a crisp dinner jacket as he told her stories about his adventures. She'd talk about her upbringing, all the traveling that they'd done, and then, they'd begin to create a list of destinations to visit together. No, she had to be focused on New York and keeping her heels firmly on the ground.

"Oh, get something to wear when you're out with your young man. I bet the pair of you are going to be following Marvin and me tonight, aren't you?"

Her cheeks flamed and she was glad Mina was in a dressing room and out of sight. "Hudson isn't my young man. And we don't follow you. We just assist in cultivating a festive and romantic atmosphere for all of our esteemed guests."

"Well, if you're going to assist, I need you to dress the part. And who knows, maybe when Hudson sees you in this dress, he'll assist you straight into a dance." There was laughter in her voice. "Go on, find something spectacular. I won't pick a dress until you do."

Nat appreciated Mina's good mood and found it almost catching. It was so different than the quiet and reserved woman she'd seen so far. That note had made her giddy.

And that attitude, it warmed Nat's heart. She supposed there was nothing wrong with getting a special dress, especially if it was going to make Mina happy. She'd already planned on staying late to ensure the salsa night went well. Why not dress the part?

"Okay," Nat said as she stood up. "You twisted my arm. I'll find something to wear, all right?"

"Perfect, and Natalie, make sure you pick it out with Hudson in mind. I think when you plan your outfit with a man in mind, it means more when he tells you you're beautiful."

Instead of correcting her again, Nat began perusing the racks, looking for something she loved. And maybe something he'd love. Nat flipped through the dresses, trying not to stress about her Hudson concerns. It was just a dress.

Then she went into the dressing room beside Mina's. While she went above and beyond for all of her guests, she had never tried on outfits in order to fit in or trailed a married couple as they worked on reviving their marriage. That was certainly a new one, and she wasn't sure exactly how she felt. It seemed like time and attendance fraud if she were being honest. She was shopping for herself while on the clock. But then again, if Mr. Sutton were here, she knew he'd allow this. Well, she'd use her own credit card and not the resort's to buy the dress. It would help with the awkwardness she felt.

The last dress in the pile didn't look like much on the

hanger, sort of shapeless and dull. She was sure she was going to pick another losing outfit. But when she put it on and inspected herself in the floor length mirror in the dressing room, she was beyond pleasantly surprised. The red wasn't bright, nor was it dull as she first thought. It had three-quarter-length sleeves and a deep V-neck. The butter-soft fabric hugged her torso, then flared out, leaving the hem to float just above her knees. She twirled from one side to the other, admiring the way it danced around her thighs.

"Did you find anything?" Mina called from outside the dressing room.

"I think so."

"Oh, let me see!"

"Okay, one moment."

Nat opened the door slowly. Mina was dressed in her regular clothes again, much to Nat's disappointment, but she didn't have much time to think about it, as Mina clapped her hands.

"Natalie, you're a vision," Mina breathed. "You have to get it."

"I might be a little overdressed at the lodge if I walk in wearing this."

"It's always better to be overdressed than underdressed. Now, get changed. We have to get back to the lodge, so I have enough time to finish getting ready before my date."

"Oh, did you find a dress?"

"Yes, I did."

"Let me see," Nat said.

"You'll see it tonight."

Nat smiled as Mina floated over to the shoe section and went back inside her dressing room. The woman looked so blissfully excited to be going out with her own husband, it gave Nat new hope that she and Hudson were doing the right thing. Maybe they weren't sticking their noses where they didn't belong. Maybe they truly were meant to help the Kents.

The salsa night would go off without a hitch, she just knew it. Rebecca had confirmed the florist had delivered the roses, Terry was making a feast of *arroz con pollo*, yuca, *croquetas*, and *pastelitos*. And for dessert, she was whipping up some flan. The dance instructor would be there at a quarter to seven, and one of the staff event workers was setting up the sound system with a dance playlist.

She was feeling so secure in her planning, she didn't need to stay all night. In fact, she didn't really need to "assist" with the dancing lesson. She'd probably just be a distraction. But as she left the dressing room, her new dress slung over one arm, she didn't want to go home. She wanted to wear her dress, and even more than that, she wanted Hudson to see her in it.

Armed with a new confidence and excitement for the evening, Nat wandered over to the shoe section. She needed to complete her outfit.

Hudson

HUDSON CHECKED HIS watch again. It was nearly seven, and still Nat was nowhere to be seen. She had texted him around five to say she was with Mina, but he expected her to be micromanaging each individual rose petal. Instead, one of her staff, a nice girl named Rebecca, seemed to be taking charge of the final setup.

The study had been closed off to guests, and it was transformed. The fire was going, and instead of reading lamps, candles had been placed on the mantel, a few of the low tables, and the larger one draped in white fabric where Terry would serve dinner. Crystal vases held roses in full bloom but nearly every flat surface and a space in the center of the room had been cleared out for the salsa lesson.

The instructor, a tall man named Marco, was flicking through the song choices with the tech who had changed the music for the night. And beside Hudson stood Marvin, looking nervous as all get out in a deep red button-down shirt with black slacks and a dark tie. Hudson thought he cleaned up pretty good, then felt he should clean up a little bit too. He quickly left and ditched his daytime clothes of hiking pants and a thermal shirt in favor of one of the things he kept in the back of his Jeep, for a situation where he might need to look a little nice. He'd changed into a pale blue button-down shirt, with the sleeves rolled to the elbow and some pressed black pants he only wore when absolutely necessary. Marvin had insisted Hudson looked sharp, but Hudson felt a little silly. It's not like he needed to dress up for her or for the dancing. Yet, here he was, in a dress shirt for the first time in months. He had to unbutton the first two buttons so he would be a little less constricted.

Hudson felt a bit like Nat, all buttoned up and ironed. He could clean up when he wanted to and knew fifteen different ways to shine a dress shoe to regulation, but it didn't mean he relished it. He felt more at home dressed for the outdoors and not a board meeting. And even though Marvin had pushed him to wear a tie, Hudson couldn't bring himself to even consider it. To him, he was going above and beyond in the fashion department.

"What time is it?" Marvin asked for the fourth time since coming downstairs.

"You know, Mina said something about you losing things all the time. I'm beginning to think she was right. I saw you wearing a watch today. What happened to it?"

"Probably in the room. I don't know, Mina usually handles that."

Hudson shook his head. "Almost seven."

"She's coming, right?"

"Why wouldn't she?"

"I don't know. Maybe she thought it was a silly idea. Possibly that we're too old for this."

Hudson put a hand on his shoulder and squeezed. It was clear Marvin was spiraling with the nerves, and he didn't want him to completely fall apart. "Take a deep breath. Tonight is all about just having fun and getting back to what you guys used to love doing together. There aren't any judges or a studio audience to cheer for you. Come on, let's go wait in the lobby, so you can escort her from the elevator."

"Yes, I can do that." Marvin nodded as if affirming he was doing the right thing.

As Hudson led the way out of the study and through the lobby, he wondered what it was like to be so nervous to see a girl, especially one you've known for years. Was that love? Getting so twisted up after being apart for a day that you turned into a mess like Marvin? He liked to think he was a little more put together than that, but what did he know?

The elevator doors opened with a ding and Marvin straightened. But it wasn't Mina, it was just a couple with two little boys who looked dressed for a swim in the indoor pool before bed. It was now just after seven, a very un-Nat thing. Then he had the sickening thought that maybe Mina didn't want to go dancing and Nat was so busy trying to convince her to come that she didn't realize what time it was. If Mina didn't show, Hudson had no idea what could possibly be done to bring the pair back together.

"Wow." Marvin's voice was low, nearly a sigh.

Hudson looked around to see what had caught his attention, and his gaze swept up the double staircase that framed the elevators. Mina was slowly descending, dressed in a black dress with fringe at the bottom that danced with every step. She was absolutely radiant, and it was clear why Marvin was speechless. And then, from behind Mina, he saw Nat. It was Hudson's turn to be speechless.

Nat's slender hand was on the banister as she walked. In the warm glow of the chandelier, he could only see her in that red dress, as if he'd zoomed in on just her. Nat's hair was loose around her shoulders in big waves. He dropped his gaze to her feet, smiling at the strappy gold high heels. Hudson had seen her in every shade of suit and skirt in existence, and she looked great in all of them, but nothing could compare to the sight of her coming toward him wearing a dress like that and a smile reserved only for him. A real smile.

He was still staring when Nat came beside him, her cheeks rosy and her eyes gleaming in the light. "Doesn't she look great?"

"Doesn't who look what?" Hudson didn't have a single idea what Nat was talking about.

She frowned and whispered, "Mina. Look at Marvin's face. I can tell he's obviously smitten."

Hudson snapped out of his haze and glanced over his shoulder. Marvin was positively beaming with delight as he made Mina do a twirl for him to show off the dress. It was a nice sight, but he would much rather look at Nat.

"Yeah, she looks good."

"Only good?" Nat crossed her arms and cocked her head to the side. "I'll have you know I spent hours with her picking out the perfect outfit and getting her ready at the spa. If she just looks good, I obviously didn't do my job."

"Trust me, Marvin is thrilled to see her. He was a wreck waiting for you guys to come down. He was actually worried she wouldn't show." He wanted to say something about her and her dress. He wanted to tell her she looked pretty, gorgeous, spectacular, all the buzz words he'd heard in movies and read in books. No matter which one he thought of, none seemed enough. But he couldn't stay silent; that would be foolish. "Nat, you look...." He couldn't even finish the sentence. He just waved his hand up and down her body, and then settled his gaze on her beautiful eyes.

Nat gave him an odd look he couldn't quite place but smiled all the same and said, "Finish your sentence, Hudson. Use your words."

And then the nerves were gone. He loved the little quips she threw at him. Though she was standing before him, flawless, she was still Nat. "Begging for compliments, are you? Alright, I cave." He reached out and took her hand, kissing her knuckles. "You're beautiful." He let go of her hand gently and slipped a stray hair behind her ear. "There, and now you're perfect."

"Thanks, Hudson," she said, dropping her eyes to the floor for a second. Then she looked back up at him. "Not so bad yourself. I'm impressed. I didn't know you owned a button-down shirt."

"Don't get used to it. This was probably a one-time thing."

"Shame, it suits you." Then she flipped her hair over her shoulder and walked over to where the Kents were standing, still gazing at one another.

As he watched Nat walk to the study, Hudson was instantly regretting his earlier decision. Marvin was right. He should have written some sort of note, just in case she showed up looking beautiful in a dress. That made him want to take *her* dancing.

"Hudson, are you coming?" Nat called out. The Kents were already headed toward the study, but she was still waiting for him. She could've been calling him to his death at that moment and he'd have followed her.

"Think we did good?" he asked with a nod in their direction.

"Between your brilliant ideas and my attention to detail, I think we pulled off some pretty awesome things."

He grinned. "You're saying I'm brilliant?"

"I believe I said your ideas were brilliant. Let's not get carried away." She held up her finger. "Remember to be on your best behavior. If you're good, Terry might have some *pastelitos* with your name on them."

"Are you bribing me with food like a dog?"

"I don't know. Is it working?"

"Like a charm."

Nat giggled, an actual giggle. It was such a light sound, he could hardly picture it coming from her lips. "Okay, time to be professional."

Marco the dance instructor greeted Mina and Marvin as Hudson and Nat tucked themselves away in a cozy alcove flanked by two bookcases. While they had a fairly clear view of Mina and Marvin, they were blissfully out of the way. In any other situation, Hudson would ask why he needed to be there. After all, Marco was taking care of the dancing and Terry was taking care of the cooking. But with Nat next to him tapping her toe to the music as she swayed in her armchair, he thanked his lucky stars he happened to be in the lobby when Mr. Sutton came to the lodge that day.

"Isn't she such a good dancer?" Nat whispered, leaning toward Hudson.

Hudson watched Marvin nearly tread on her feet. "Someone in the relationship needs to have some rhythm."

"Are you a good dancer?"

"I'm much better at rock climbing and free diving than I am on a dance floor, but I feel like whoever my partner was would be less likely to end up with a broken foot than others."

"Well that doesn't inspire confidence."

"Only one way to find out." Hudson stood and held out his hand. "Come on. If we're gonna hang out all night, we might as well learn a few salsa moves."

"You have to be joking."

"Is this the face of a man who would joke about something as serious as salsa?"

Nat looked at him blankly, then nodded. "Yeah, you fit the bill."

"I can be serious if I want to. Come on, Nat, dance with me. If you think I'm being ridiculous, you can step on my foot and never dance with me again, okay?"

Her gaze flitted from his outstretched hand to his face and back again. "I don't know if this is a good idea. We've already missed the basics."

"Then we'll make them up. Trust me, I have a pretty expansive imagination."

"Oh, what the heck. Let's give it a try."

"Don't strain yourself with excitement."

"I'll do my best."

As soon as she rose from her seat, Hudson pulled her into his arms before he could lose his nerve. The action caught her by surprise, and her hazel eyes widened. He'd been paying close attention to Marco's instructions for the first three songs, although it wasn't exactly a beginners' class, since the Kents were no strangers to salsa, despite what Marvin's lack of rhythm seemed to suggest. When he was holding Mina, she took charge and he managed to follow along. But Hudson had been forced to learn the waltz for different country club functions when he'd been home. He had some basic skills. If Nat could follow lead, they'd be in a good place.

He placed one hand on the swell of her hip as he held her fingers tightly in the other. She rested her palm on his shoulder, and they gently moved to the song, which was a bit faster than he would have liked. It would have been easier if the Kents were into ballroom dancing and not the electric, exciting beat of salsa. Still, he didn't want to give up.

"Hold on tight, I'm going to spin you," he said, keeping one eye on Marco as he instructed the Kents. It was a good thing Hudson was a fast learner.

With one hand, he spun Nat out then pulled her back in, her back against his chest. He was thrilled that had actually worked and they hadn't ended up flying into a bookcase of mystery novels. Maybe if running a Spartan Gym didn't work out, he could take up dance. Marco was fit. It'd probably keep Hudson in good shape and there was probably less of a chance he'd injure himself.

As Marco corrected the Kents' footwork, Hudson and Nat mirrored their moves, grinning to each other in the candlelit dimness of their alcove. With each part of the lesson, they both became a little bolder, a little more open with their clumsy steps and loose turns that would probably have Marco snapping his fingers to correct them if he saw.

Hudson spun Nat, pulling her in close to him. Looking down into her eyes, he began to wonder. She'd put up a fight about dancing but was in a salsa dress. What was she expecting to happen? "Nat, why'd you wear that dress?"

"What?" she asked, pulling away from him a bit. "As opposed to what? Overalls?"

"No, sorry, that didn't come out right. Did you expect to dance with me?"

She shrugged, turning away to watch the Kents. Hudson stayed quiet, allowing her to sort out her answer.

"Well," she finally said. "I guess I wanted to be ready just in case."

His throat grew tight. It wasn't exactly a confession of feelings, but it was certainly something he could savor. "I'm glad you did."

Nat's phone chirped from the purse on the armchair then she scrambled to silence it. She took it from her purse and held it to her ear, one hand cupped over the mouthpiece, as she had a whispered conversation, Hudson trying to figure out if his words of affirmation would have actually gone anywhere if the phone hadn't rung. And where exactly would he want them to go? What if that slot in California opened and he decided to go for it? In theory, distance sounded easy enough if you really cared about the other person, but distance bred resentment, something he saw more than enough every time he left his parents' home in California to go to boarding school.

"That was Terry," Nat explained as she put the phone back into her purse. "She was just warning me that they were coming with dinner."

"Is this the part where I get my *pastelitos*?" He tried to

sound jovial, but he was a little annoyed that the call had ruined the moment they had been sharing.

"I guess we'll see. I'll have to ask Terry."

"Good thing I'm her favorite then."

Nat rolled her eyes. "You wish." Then she shouldered her purse and edged out the study to slip out the doors with Hudson close behind. It seemed like Marco was wrapping up the lessons, which was fine, since as soon as they stepped out of the study, they were surrounded with delicious scents he couldn't even place.

Terry was standing in the hall with a rolling cart with a number of silver domed plates. "How are the two lovebirds?"

"I think it's going really well," Nat said eagerly. "Hudson and I watched from the corner and they haven't fought or given each other nasty looks all night."

"Well, what is it they say about music, it soothes all?"

"They also say the way to a man's heart is through his stomach so between your food and the dance, they should leave even more in love." Nat reached out to lift one of the lids.

Terry slapped Nat's hand away. "I did not spend hours slaving over a hot stove to prepare this immaculate meal only for you to serve it. I will be the only one touching these dishes tonight."

"Fine, that's fair enough."

"Hey, Terry, Nat said you might have a little something for me?" Hudson said, trying to put on a charming smile.

"I have a lot of some things for you, but nothing on this cart right now."

"That's okay, I'm willing to take a walk down to the kitchen."

"Wrong direction," Terry said. "I set up a few plates in the cafe. It closed at seven thirty, so you'll be nice and out of the way." Then she winked at Hudson at an angle Nat couldn't have possibly seen. "Well, I should get in there and start serving. Now go eat the food I made you two before it gets cold."

Nat looked worried. "But what about the Kents? I can't just leave them."

"They are grown adults, not untrained puppies. Have a nice night." Then Terry slipped through the open study doors and promptly shut them behind her.

Nat paused for only a moment before grabbing Hudson's arm. "Come on, we can go in the back way."

Hudson planted his feet. "Terry just said she made me a lot of some things. Do you really think I'm going to go watch those people eat when I could be sampling some of her delicious cooking? You really don't know me at all, do you?"

"This is important."

"Really, things are going so smoothly. We can go get some well-deserved dinner, then swing past the study again later to see if they're still there. Best-case scenario they were too busy staring into each other's eyes over a candlelit dessert to even notice our existence."

"Well, I guess you're right."

"Let's go before you change your mind."

Hudson instinctively took her hand and was pleased when her fingers slipped through his. From the outside, they were a well-dressed couple, maybe guests at the lodge who had just come back from a romantic night out. They fit the role of newlyweds on a honeymoon or maybe a couple celebrating an anniversary. He could see it in the smiles of guests as they passed, who probably didn't recognize Nat outside her suits, and probably didn't know Hudson at all. The looks they gave them made Hudson's chest swell with pride. He liked having a beautiful, smart woman like Nat on his arm. And if the dinner was anything like the one Terry had sorted for the Kents, Hudson would owe her big-time. And maybe not just for the food.

Nat

NAT STILL FELT like she was dancing. When she woke up that morning, the last place she thought she would be that night was walking through the halls of Hazel Oaks, holding Hudson's hand, on their way to a surprise dinner. When she had talked to Terry earlier, all she asked was maybe that she put aside a few snacks for them, not a full meal. But by the look Terry had given her as she left her office, it was clear her friend had some tricks up the sleeve of her chef's coat that Nat couldn't even dream of.

The lights inside the cafe were off, and a sign in the glass store read closed. But there was still a glow emanating from within. Hudson pushed the door experimentally and then opened it all the way when he realized it wasn't locked.

The cafe was a fairly new installation, once a smaller restaurant, now a cozy place for couples and families to enjoy cups of hot chocolate and coffee and decadent baked goods like macaroons and gooey chocolate chip cookies. Meant to keep the same feel of the lodge, the walls were exposed wood and the love seats that had been set out for Valentine's Day were nearly antiques with plush velvet seating and ornate legs.

It was done up for the holiday with tasteful decor like fresh flowers that were exchanged every three days and vintage Valentine's Day cards strung up above a single small fireplace that now had a fire roaring in the hearth. The holiday may have been a few days off but Nat thought it was important to decorate in advance to get guests in the mood for the holiday.

It didn't take that long to see why Terry had seemed so pleased. A table had been brought into the cafe and set before the wall of windows overlooking the darkened lake. It was not as formal as the white cloth one in the study for the Kents, but still a lovely setup with the gold-rimmed dishes usually reserved for the guests and a crystal vase with a dozen red roses. At each setting was a silver dome covering whatever delicacies Terry had cooked for them. It was thoughtful and romantic. Nat wasn't sure what to say. She usually planned things like this for others. But she'd never experienced something as perfect as this.

So far, she had been having a wonderful night with Hudson; she was beginning to see a new, truly romantic side to him that she hadn't thought someone like him would possess. He wasn't some fabulous dancer, but he'd sent chills down her spine every time his fingers grazed her arm, or he held her a little closer. There were certainly sparks.

"Wow, Terry really outdid herself," Hudson said as he pulled out Nat's seat for her.

"She always goes above and beyond. Around Christmas last year, I invited her over to watch a few movies. She said she was going to bring us a few snacks, and three hours later, she arrived with a complete holiday dinner. I'm talking turkey, mashed potatoes, corn, rolls, the works."

"It sounds like I need to be invited to your parties." Hudson sat down and removed the domes on their plates. *Arroz con pollo*, yuca, *croquetas*, and *pastelitos* had been carefully set on the large dishes. Beside them were two smaller plates with the flan.

"This looks so delicious."

"Aren't you glad I forced you to tear yourself away from the Kents?"

"Maybe just a little," she admitted as she unfolded her

napkin and draped it across her lap.

They began eating, and a silence fell over them. Nat wasn't sure what to make of it. Of course the food was spectacular as always, but they weren't just sharing a regular meal like they had before in the employee cafeteria. This time there was candlelight and the memory of music and dancing. It was like a real date. She was in a beautiful dress and he was in a button-up shirt, and they were looking at one another over the tops of long-stemmed roses.

It made her think of the failure of a date she'd gone on with Chris from the online dating company. She had expected a night like this with him, but he'd delivered scolding and judgment. Hudson never seemed to do that. He was never harsh with her, at least not in the way that hurt. He challenged her and made her truly think about her choices and her place in everything.

"We make a good team," she said suddenly.

Hudson looked up, his fork halfway to his mouth. "Nat, I can only take so many compliments in one night before I start getting nervous you're about to tell me something terrible."

"Don't be silly. I'm just saying you and I are working really well together. I probably would have never figured out this dance thing without you."

He smiled, a soft smile that was so different than his usual impish grin. "Maybe you wouldn't but I'm sure you would've figured out something almost as good as my idea," he said.

Nat chucked a little piece of bread at him and scrunched her face up, glaring at him dramatically.

Hudson laughed and picked up the bread. "If we leave food on the floor, I have a very distinct feeling Terry will absolutely have a fit, and I have no interest in angering the lady who feeds me on a regular basis."

"Yeah, you're probably right."

"But in all seriousness, Nat, I think we make a good team too." He reached his hand out and took hers, rubbings circles on the back of it with his thumb. It was such a natural thing, so warm and familiar. "This has actually been a lot of fun. I didn't think it would be at first."

"I hope it wasn't because I gave you such a hard time at the beginning. I just...this job is important to me. Sometimes, I worry that I take it too seriously and one day it'll be all I have." As soon as the words came out Nat wanted to take them back. She pulled her hand back, then dropped her eyes and focused on her food. The thought was real, but she usually didn't think about it outside her bedroom in the middle of the night when sleep eluded her. She wanted more. She wanted someone to grow old with and to raise children with and go through all of life's joys and disasters with.

"Hey," Hudson said. "Look at me."

Nat tried to reassemble her face so the sadness she felt wouldn't be plain to see. After a few moments, she glanced up at him. His eyes were soft, but she didn't see pity. Hudson, ever the optimist, always the clown, had a bright smile that warmed her, despite the concerns regarding what she'd said. It just made her think about their hike when she'd started sharing details about her past. Something about him made her feel like she could talk to him about anything.

"Nat, you'll find it."

"How do you know?" she whispered as if she was talking to herself.

"Because I'm the romance expert here."

Nat rolled her eyes, but she couldn't keep the smile off her face either.

"Come on," Hudson said, wiping his mouth and then his hands on a napkin. He reached out a hand to her and said, "Let's dance."

"You seriously want to dance after all that food?" Nat wasn't used to eating so much, but Terry's cooking was hard to resist, and she put away much more than she thought possible.

"It's *because* of all the food that I want to dance. If I don't get moving, I will fall asleep right here on one of those love seats. Besides, our last dance was interrupted." He stood up and held his hand to her like he did in the study. "Don't tell me you already forgot everything Marco taught you tonight."

"Don't you go questioning my abilities."

"Then maybe I just want to dance with you again."

"But there's no music." She looked around trying to spot the speaker. Had Terry set one up maybe? She couldn't help but wonder if she and Hudson were in cahoots. Though, if they were, she owed her friend a car or something like that.

"Have a little faith." He slipped his phone from his back pocket, scrolled through some things, then set it on the table.

A slow song began—something classic and memorable, though Nat couldn't quite place it. Still, she and Hudson came together almost immediately, a hand on his shoulder, her fingers clasping his, his palm leaving a searing heat on her waist. She wouldn't call their dance salsa, but something a little easier, something meant for someone like her who had musical talent but whose body lacked a little in the physical rhythm department. Her two left feet wouldn't allow for anything too challenging.

She wondered if the Kents had nearly as nice a night as she had. And then she decided to stop thinking about them. This moment wasn't about the Kents. She needed to realize they would be alright, and no matter what she and Hudson did, the only people who could save their marriage was them. She needed to try and see everything else going on around her...or perhaps what was going on right in front of her.

Nat looked up into Hudson's eyes and inched a little closer to him. It'd been so long since she'd gone on a good date that left her filled with butterflies and the delicious sensation of hope. And while the night didn't start as a date, it sure felt like one. It was one of the most enjoyable evenings she'd had in a very long time. He wasn't some immature jokester...well, he was, but he was also a complicated man with deeper thoughts and emotions than she expected. That made her feel immature that she had judged him so harshly. In reality he used his infectious moods for the power of good, often making her smile even when she didn't think she could.

After the fourth song in a row, with her head now resting on his shoulder, the music stopped altogether, and their footsteps stilled. Her heart was beating so loudly, she wondered if Hudson could hear it. Although they were no longer dancing, he was still holding her tight. She lifted her head from his shoulder and looked up at him. Hudson was draped in candle and firelight, his angular features had been softened, and his pale eyes glowed in the dark. He was just as handsome as she'd been fantasizing.

Nat instinctively tilted her chin upward as he leaned in, and her eyes closed just as his lips found hers in the softest of kisses. It was a fleeting moment, but her entire body flickered with the excitement of a first kiss. It had been gentle and unexpected, though not unwelcome, and Nat nearly pulled him back down for another as his mouth left hers.

"It's nearly eleven," Hudson said in a low voice, his face inches from hers.

"Oh, I suppose it is rather late. I have an early start in the morning."

"Me too, although I won't be at work. It's my day off."

Nat felt a pang of disappointment, because she wouldn't see Hudson the next day. "I guess I should have noticed your name wasn't on the schedule for tomorrow."

"What a very un-Natalie type thing of you." He placed a hand on her forehead. "You feel okay? You don't have a fever."

She laughed and turned her face away. "I've had a lot on my mind."

"Anything I can help you with? I'm quite the listener. Ask Marvin. He can vouch for me."

Nat didn't know what to say. There were so many feelings swirling around in her head, especially now that they kissed. But as she considered saying something to him, expressing some of these feelings, she decided not to. She needed to stop thinking and overanalyzing everything, and just bask in this moment.

"No, not now. Let's just start a song over and have one last dance."

Hudson walked over to his phone and fiddled with it. "Well, my phone is dead. Where's yours?"

"In my office."

"Then I guess we're done for the night."

"Should we bring these dishes to the kitchen?"

"No, Terry told me housekeeping would take care of it."

"So efficient."

"She's the best."

A silent, awkward feeling settled over them like a cloud,

hazy and cold. Nat wasn't sure what to do with the new sensation. A few moments ago, they'd shared a kiss, and now there was a sort of stilted politeness between them. She wanted to slip back into the easy comfort they had shared over dinner, but she was too shy to make the first move. She had always known Hudson was braver than she ever would be. But just this once, she was going to do something. Nat reached out and took his hand as they left the cafe.

It was quiet as Nat and Hudson walked down the hall toward the employee exit. Hudson didn't even give her a hard time when she turned left instead of right, merely followed her down the hall. It was almost strange interacting with Hudson without the constant teasing, but she was enjoying this new side of him where she didn't have to constantly have a sharp retort on the tip of her tongue. She just wished they could recapture the sparks they felt when they kissed.

He went so far as to walk her to her office, where she grabbed her things, and then to the car. As they stood outside her car, with her keys in her hand, she still wasn't ready to get in it. Once she did, the night was over. Nat wanted to say something to him, something to make him laugh, maybe for him to kiss her again.

"Hudson, I had a really good time tonight," she said.

"I did too." He reached a hand out and touched her cheek, then slid it behind her neck gently, pulling her to him as he kissed her again. He leaned back, taking her breath with him. "I guess I'll see you later," he said and then turned to head back to the resort.

He seemed almost distracted, like there was something he'd forgotten to do. She'd never seen him like that, and she wasn't sure if it was a good thing or a bad thing where she was involved. Did he not mean to kiss her again? Did he already regret whatever closeness they shared?

She dug her keys out of her purse not entirely sure what to make of everything. He walked off without a look back. He had kissed her and then ran back inside, leaving her a confused mess. Instead of his soft kiss on her lips, she had questions. That whole basking in the moment thing didn't work. Nat tried to brush off how the night ended and focus on the good parts. She turned the music on in the car, finding a slow song to reminisce.

CHAPTER EIGHT

Hudson

HUDSON BARELY GOT any sleep that night. The kiss was imprinted in his mind. The spark he'd felt threatening to burn him alive. He'd felt something for her. Something right. He just had no idea how to act. He dated girls, took them out for nights on the town, to movies and dinner. But she was different. He wouldn't take her out three times and then decide they'd be better as friends or tell her after two dates that there was a spark missing.

From his first day, she had been the untouchable queen of the resort. Whatever she said was law when it came to her staff, and even the staff and other departments respected her hard work and dedication. The first time he saw her, she had been dressed in a black pencil skirt and a pale pink silk blouse. She'd been sitting in one of the conference rooms alone, a pile of notebooks stacked before her. He hadn't known who she was and had leaned against the doorway and given her one of his most charming grins. Then he made a joke about how much of a stickler for rules he heard the head concierge was and how he was excited to shake things up a bit, hoping to bond over a mutual frustration.

The gorgeous strawberry blonde gave him a brilliant smile, collected her notebooks, and brushed past him. "She really is. I bet she won't like you a single bit. Have fun." On her way through the door, she had passed him her business card. It read *Natalie Keller, Head Concierge.*

They didn't see much of each other during the first few weeks he worked there. Hudson spent a great deal of time training and learning the resort with the other adventure coordinators, and Nat was inside doing various administrative things or ducking in and out of the other offices to coordinate dinners and outings. She'd come out to the lobby to handle the guests every now and then. He'd watch her make her way through the room, chatting with everyone, checking on their stays, making notes in her notebook, handing out pamphlets. It was clear she loved her job just maybe not as clear how the two of them would ever find something in common. So in general, even when he was in the resort, he stayed out of her way.

But it had soon proved to be unavoidable. He'd need to talk to her about a guest or give her a briefing on a new activity he wanted to plan. She'd have schedule questions or special guest requests. And with those moments, the teasing started, the witty remarks passed back and forth as they saw each other. He always admired her quick wit. No one seemed to be able to put him in his place quite as quickly and thoroughly as Natalie Keller. And it always surprised him when it happened because it was like seeing a crack in a porcelain doll. She wasn't just a customer service robot. Then, he just enjoyed joking with her.

Now things were vastly different. He was allowed to call her Nat, hold her hand, even kiss her. After golf he'd dreamt about holding her again, about what it might be like to travel with her. She seemed like the kind of girl he could take trekking up a mountain or hang gliding. As long as he put it on the schedule, she'd probably do it. And that was exactly the kind of woman he always wanted. And then as he was dressing for the dance lessons he started thinking about other opportunities to be together. Real ones. Tangible ones. Like, he wanted to go to the wishing well and get some professional pictures taken for the website. Nat would have the perfect eye for that. He was going to the gym today and he wondered if Nat would want to give one of their workouts a try. Hudson wanted to take her camping out in a giant field. They'd lie out, staring at the stars as she told him all the stories of her life, about playing violin in Germany, moving to Spain as a kid, how she decided Hazel Oaks was the place she would plant her roots.

He'd even considered what it would be like if she ever met his family. Though, to be honest, he quit on that thought quickly since it seemed to set off anxiety he didn't know he had. That must've been the reason his heart pounded so rapidly when he'd pondered that idea for the briefest of seconds.

Each time he saw Nat, he learned more about her. With each new discovery he was realizing just how perfect she really could be for him. She had this structure he hated and yet somehow needed. But she also wanted to take some time and be a little wild and free, traveling the globe, making friends wherever she stopped. She loved exercise and seemed to thrive outside. All things that left his head spinning, yet he craved more. She wasn't just quick-witted and pretty, she was whip-smart and had the kind of upbringing that both mirrored and contrasted his.

As he did his morning workout in the Spartan Gym, he couldn't seem to turn off his mind, no matter how loudly he turned his music up or how heavy the tires he flipped were. Usually, he relished his days off to try out some obstacles or do some hiking and exploring around the rest of Lake George. But he had no interest in giving the newly installed rope course behind the gym a spin. All he really wanted to do was have a cup of coffee in Nat's office and tease her as she flipped through her color-coordinated notebooks in search of the perfect lunch appetizer.

How many notebooks did that woman own? She seemed to have one for everything. Hudson was never a great gift giver, but at least he knew Natalie would always appreciate a new one of those.

He was wondering if she would like a plain color or pattern for a new notebook when the owner of the gym, Ben, came out of the office. He made a beeline for Hudson, who pulled out his earbuds as he approached.

"Hey there, you're here later than usual for your day off," Ben said as he sat on the weight bench beside him.

"Yeah, I had a late night."

"Hot date?"

Hudson took a long drink from his water bottle, debating on how much to reveal. "Something like that."

"So, you met someone? I guess I don't have to send you an invite to the single's mixer."

"To be honest, I've known her for a while."

Ben studied him, and then asked, "Is it that pretty brunette who lives in your building?"

"No. Hannah is pretty, but I wasn't really interested."

"Oh. Okay, then who is it? Do I know her?"

Hudson considered how much to tell him. Ben didn't know Nat and would probably never meet her, so there wasn't much harm in telling him who we had spent his evening with. Still, he wasn't exactly sure how to classify their evening together. He would like to call it a date, but was it really just a work function? Work functions never ended in a kiss, in his estimation.

"It was with this woman, Natalie…Nat. We were working on a project together and had some dinner."

"If it was just a basic dinner, you shouldn't be killing yourself right now."

"Aren't you supposed to be off training somebody or

something?"

"Lucky for you, they said they're running late. I'm all yours. What did you do?"

"We just had dinner and did some salsa dancing. Nothing exciting. I mean, the weather is terrible so we couldn't go skydiving or anything too fun."

Ben grinned. "I didn't know you could dance."

"I am a man of many talents, many skills, and two left feet. She was no pro either, so it ended up alright. I did get a kiss though, so she must not have hated my dancing that much."

"Look at you, nailing down a date for Valentine's Day. Do you have anything special planned?"

There was that word again. Date. The word itself was innocuous, but what it meant was something more. Dates meant relationships, relationships meant roots, roots meant being tied to one place. "Nothing as of yet."

"Come on, man, it's only a week away."

"Yeah? Then what are you doing for Paula?"

Ben had been dating Paula for nearly two years, and Hudson wouldn't be surprised if they ended up tying the knot sooner rather than later.

"I have it all planned out. Brunch at her favorite spot in the morning, then part of the day at her favorite museum, then home to get changed into something fancy, then dinner at this Michelin star restaurant. I've preordered two dozen pink roses, her favorite, and bought the classic teddy bear and chocolate combo."

Hudson was torn. He wasn't doing that, but he and Nat weren't dating. Though, he certainly didn't kiss any of his other coworkers. He wasn't sure if he should plan a night out, or give her chocolates and a bear, or maybe a notebook with chocolates and a bear printed on it.

"Are my grand romantic gestures making you feel inadequate?" Ben asked with a laugh.

"No way, there's just a lot going on. The big boss of the lodge is sort of counting on me for something, and I don't want to mess it up. Besides, this girl isn't a casual dater. She's the bring home to Mom type. And we work together." He leaned forward, draping his arms over his knees. "I don't know, man. It just feels good, you know, when I'm with her and all. Then I leave and I'm doubting everything. Plus, I'm trying to get to California soon. What am I gonna do? Just leave her in the dust?"

"You mean like you'll be doing to all the people you've met here? All the friends and connections you've made at this gym?"

Hudson swung his legs off the leg press and turned to look at Ben. It was true. He hadn't really considered that all his California talk over the last few weeks was probably insensitive. He would be leaving his friends. Not just Ben, but several others. To him, it was normal, just part of his fear of being stuck somewhere for too long. He'd kept in touch with friends he'd made from the previous gyms he'd worked in. Even saw a lot of them at various obstacle course competitions. But it would never be like seeing them regularly at the gym. Training together really established bonds.

"I told you, I'd be a partner in a gym over there. Plus, my buddies want to start some Spartan races and really, I'd be able to design my own course. Set my name in the sport."

"I know, man. I get it. I'm just saying, we'll miss you. I'm sure this girl will too. From the looks of you, I'd guess she's not the only one who enjoyed the dancing and dinner."

"I just worry I'm not being fair to her, but then, I guess I don't want to stay away from her either."

"It seems to me you have a couple options. You don't have your bag packed for California yet, so why not see where things go with her? Or stop talking to her because something might happen."

"Was psychology a prerequisite for your kinesiology degree?" Hudson asked, trying to lighten up the conversation. It was getting too serious for him. All the discussions of moving and the job possibilities had him on edge. He hadn't even been offered the job in California yet. He'd need it while the gym became profitable.

"Yes. I can do mind and body training. I'm special that way."

Hudson shook his head and grabbed a pair of dumbbells and started curling. The forty-fives weren't giving him the burn he wanted so he put them back down and upped the weight to fifty.

"Bro, seriously, you need to slow down. This girl's gonna give you an injury."

"Yeah, I know."

HE RETURNED TO the lodge after his day off unsure exactly how to proceed with Nat. He hadn't called or texted after he left. Hudson had started to a few times but never went through with it. Originally, he'd been worried what she'd think about dating a coworker. Now, he wasn't sure what *he* thought about dating one. He really wasn't sure of anything.

So Hudson walked into the resort and headed straight for his office. He went over his schedule there, checked his email, and then sat in his chair ignoring the rumble in his stomach. If he went in the kitchen, he'd see Terry. She'd want to know all about the dinner, though, she'd probably already gotten all the details from Nat. Honestly, he'd be surprised if the chef wasn't already planning the dinner options for their wedding...that is if Nat had spoken of their evening favorably. There was a chance she'd woken up the next day and vowed to never so much as look at him again. He needed to lay low and see what happened.

But he couldn't hide long. There was a knock on his open door. He spun his chair around and was face-to-face with Nat. She was dressed in a white blouse and a red pencil skirt that mimicked the color of her lipstick. Her hair was pulled back in some complicated knot that made her look like one of the sophisticated ladies at a country club. But her smile, it was her smile that nearly broke him. It wasn't a courtesy smile, her standard, "hey, how are you doing this morning?" smile. She was happy to see specifically him. And, if he were honest, five minutes ago he'd been dreading seeing her. Now that she was here, he couldn't imagine getting through the day without the scent of her floral perfume or hearing her ridiculous laugh that made her sound like both a Disney princess and an out-of-control child at the same time.

"Nat, hey. Has anyone told you, red is a good color on you?"

Her cheeks blushed, the pink clashing with her lipstick. "Has anyone told you flattery is the way to a girl's heart?"

"No, actually, I was told diamonds, but I'm glad to know I don't have to worry about that with you."

"No, not diamonds. I'm an emerald girl. Unique but classic."

"Well, I'll keep that in mind. Add it to my romantic dossier."

"You do that," she said and then looked down at her clipboard. "Um, on another note for your romantic dossier. It's for Operation Valentine," she said. He chuckled a little. She'd used the code name. He loved it.

"I thought about your little morning hike with the Johnsons and watching the sunrise and all that. I wondered, with the Kents, is there some place you could drive them to in order to watch the sunset? Mina mentioned to me that the hike was a little hard on Marvin's knees, but I think they'd enjoy a peaceful moment like that alone. Maybe there's some place you could drive them to?" She looked at him expectantly, as if he was supposed to produce a list right then and there.

"Yeah, um, I'd have to scout a couple places. Did it need to be today?"

"Oh, no, it could be tomorrow or the next day. I was just thinking of things for them." And then she looked down at her clipboard again. "You know, if you'd like, I have a free afternoon. We could go together, if you wanted a woman's opinion."

"Yeah, you should definitely come." The words escaped from his mouth before his brain could catch up. Part of him wanted nothing more than to spend the afternoon with her. Just the two of them looking for a romantic sunset location. It'd be a no-brainer. But then again, all the worries from yesterday and his chat with Ben were screaming loudly in his ear. He couldn't keep riding this line. Hudson needed to figure out what he wanted to do. Did he want to really try something with Nat? Did he want to say, not a good time, and end things before he moved, or things got too serious, or they broke up, causing tension at work?

Well, maybe spending the afternoon together would help him make a decision. He'd use the short trip to figure out exactly what he wanted. With the two of them taking time alone, it was perfect.

"Can you meet me out front at one?" he asked, glancing at his schedule to see when he'd be free.

"Fantastic. I have an appointment in ten, so I have to go. See you later?"

"Can't wait."

Nat

NAT WORKED THOUGH lunch so that she'd be able to spend the afternoon alone with Hudson without too many calls from her staff or guests. Of course, she could end up not having service and the point would be moot, but she didn't want to ignore her work just to have some fun. Rebecca insisted she could handle the lodge, and she was a great employee. It was time to loosen the reigns.

In her head, she saw Hudson taking her down a tiny off-road path where they'd pull into a clearing surrounded by lavender plants. He'd help her out of the big Jeep he'd naturally be driving, lifting her out of the car and placing her delicately on the ground as if she weighed nothing. They'd hold hands and wander to the middle of the field with blossoms brushing against her legs and the tips of her fingers. Nat would have a picnic basket expertly packed by Terry, who, Nat was beginning to think deserved a raise.

She stopped her fantasy briefly to make a note. She needed to tell Mr. Sutton how much help Terry had been with the Kents. Once she crossed her Ts on that bullet point, she went back to her daydream.

Hudson would spread out a blanket and Nat would pass out the food. In this fantasy, it wasn't terribly cold outside, so she was in her favorite blush sundress and Hudson had on a cream polo and jeans. They'd sip on glasses of champagne, nibble on some strawberries, and watch the sunset paint the purple flowers a deep violet. As it went down, they'd make a wish on the first star that popped out, both unknowingly wishing for the same thing, that the night would never end.

However, it was thirty-seven degrees outside, so she made a note to bring heated blankets with the Kents on their trip. And she made a note to take one for their scouting mission that afternoon, just in case.

Nat was about to turn off her computer and head out to meet Hudson when her phone rang. She didn't need any of her positive thoughts before she picked up the call. She felt as if she'd been smiling nonstop since Hudson had kissed her.

"This is Natalie Keller, head concierge at Hazel Oaks Resort. How may I help you?"

"Natalie, it's George Sutton again."

"Hello, Mr. Sutton, what can I do for you? Are you looking for another report on the Kents?" She hoped not. Even though they were doing well for now, and they'd loved their couple's spa day yesterday, it felt weird telling him about it. Like she was telling a parent about their child's prom night.

"Anything problematic?"

"Not that I've seen so far."

"Excellent. Not that I'm surprised. While I'm glad to hear that, it's not the only reason I called. I mentioned the wishing well to my wife and how the Kents are at Hazel Oaks, and she's decided we will be spending Valentine's Day there as well."

"Oh, that's wonderful, sir," she said with as much excitement as she could muster. Truthfully, it made her panic a little. He didn't really stay at Hazel Oaks. He usually just stopped by for a bit and then stayed at his place, The Monarch Hotel, in New York City. Well, this would certainly challenge her. And actually, she liked that idea. Let him be wowed by her excellent skills.

"I think so. It'll be a nice little romantic vacation for us. Maybe you can even book us one of those romantic type activities you're setting up for the Kents. Really do it up for her. Money is no object."

"I can do that," she said, scribbling furiously in her notebook. "And I can plan a brunch together for you and the Kents. What day are you all coming?"

"We'll be there in five days, the thirteenth."

"Understood. I'll make sure a suite is ready for you."

"Excellent. I'll see you then."

"Oh, sir, before you hang up, I wanted to tell you how

much help Terry, our head chef, has been with the Kents. She's been making them all these special and extravagant meals and many of our plans wouldn't be possible without her expertise."

"Wonderful. I'm glad to hear it. I'm sorry, we can talk more about this later. I must get on another call. Have a good day, Natalie." And like that he hung up.

"Alright then," Natalie said out loud to herself before placing the phone back in the cradle.

She finished closing up her office and grabbed her coat off the hook, daydreaming again about lavender fields and champagne kisses.

AFTER CHATTING WITH the hotel's general manager, Nat headed to the main parking lot, looking for Hudson. He was leaning against a resort Jeep, arms crossed in front of him. He was talking with one of the valets. Nat watched him for a minute as he threw back his head to laugh and slap the other guy on the back. Things with Hudson, when she relaxed a bit, were easy. But more than that, it seemed like he was like that with everyone.

He was so different from what she'd always known, from how she was raised, yet he came from a similar structure. It was crazy how differently it affected people. Yet, it was also perfect. He made her want to slow down. So today, she didn't have a schedule. She did have a couple of locations she thought they could check out if they couldn't find one, obviously. But she liked the idea of just driving around with him. Wasn't that a song, "I'd Rather Ride Around With You"? Today, that was what she wanted.

She walked over to Hudson and he turned as she got close. His face lit up when their eyes met, and she tried to remember how to walk. He just made her want to swoon. Maybe she could get some guy to follow her around with a chaise so she could dramatically fall down whenever he looked at her with that ever-familiar smolder.

"Ready to go?" he asked when she was in front of him.

"Yes," she said, sliding the duffel bag she'd packed higher up her shoulder.

"I thought you said we were leaving for the afternoon."

"We are."

"Right, so that duffel bag has a body in it we need to bury? Maybe shovels so we can dig for treasure? Oh, did Terry send food?" His face brightened with the last question, and he eyed the bag hopefully.

"Are you only nice to me because you're afraid Terry will stop feeding you?"

"Yes," he said, taking the duffel bag from her, lifting it as if it were light as a feather.

She slapped him playfully on the arm and groaned at his bad joke. She loved how strong he was, his muscles showing through just about everything he wore. Well, not the heavy winter jacket, but the blue one he was wearing now.

Once the duffel was in the Jeep, he held the door open for her and helped her into the passenger seat. She got herself situated and buckled up. It'd been forever since she'd done any off-roading, but she was still excited. It was like a mini roller coaster, except you had no idea what the track had in store for you.

Hudson climbed into the driver's seat and they were off.

Nat was familiar with most of the roads surrounding the resort, knew them like the back of her hand. But for the first time in a while, she was looking for places of beauty between the clusters of trees, and private homes, and businesses. Things were quieter in the dead of winter, softer somehow. When she took the familiar route from her apartment to Hazel Oaks, she wasn't looking for lovely places for picnics with sunset views. She was merely driving on autopilot, giving no thought to the wonders around her.

Now, that's all she could think about. She longed for flower-filled fields and hidden glens, ancient wells and fairy pools. She wanted all the things she read about in storybooks and saw in movies. It seemed such a childish thing to wish for her, but Hudson made her long for it. He made her want the kind of romance that only existed in movies and books, which seemed a heavy load to give someone else to bear, but she couldn't help it. Nat wanted him to be that person.

"So, seriously, what's in the bag?" he asked after they'd driven a few miles.

"Terry did send us with a snack. I wasn't sure how long this would take, and I don't think there'll be any fast-food restaurants or convenience stores if we end up somewhere in the woods."

"Very true."

"And I brought a blanket, in case it's cold and some flashlights; just that kinda thing."

"It's cute, this preparedness thing, but where do you think we're going?"

"I don't know, hence the bag."

"Alright. Whatever you say."

A soft silence fell between them. To Nat, it felt a little awkward, something she hadn't expected. She'd gotten very used to him filling the quiet moments with jokes and teasing. Just two nights before, he had his arms wrapped around her and his lips on hers, yet there they were, exchanging small talk like they were strangers.

And just then, Nat realized that in many ways, they truly were strangers. She'd learned a lot of surface things in their time together, but there hadn't been any earth-shattering revelations. She wasn't really sure of his favorite color or his favorite food. Was he afraid of anything? Did he have a pet? What was his favorite holiday?

"Let's play a game while you drive," she suggested, turning a little in her seat to look at him.

"What kind of game?"

"It's a fun one."

"I'm skeptical."

"Hey, I'm the head concierge at Hazel Oaks Resort, I know how to have fun."

"Alright, fun master, what's the game?"

"I'm going to tell you something most people don't know about me and then you're going to do the same. We don't really know much about each other, and now that we're alone in the car and not on babysitting duty, I thought, why not take this opportunity."

Hudson was nodding his head lightly as she was talking, but he didn't respond to her right away. She watched him, waiting to see if there was some change in his face to possibly reveal how he was feeling. His lips didn't purse so he didn't look annoyed or irritated. His eyebrows didn't raise in silent judgment. His eyes didn't bulge out in shock. No, everything was neutral as he concentrated.

"Okay, let's do it," he finally answered.

She mulled over a few facts about herself, then said, "When I was in fourth grade, I was so in love with Aaron Carter from the Backstreet Boys that I wrote him a letter every night for a year. He never responded to a single one."

"In your honor I'm going to have to root for NSYNC in the best boy band competition from now on. The nerve of that guy."

Nat laughed. "I know. I still can't believe I did it. Anyway, your turn."

"Let's see. I won the push-up competition at school all four years I entered."

"That's cheating. Everyone at your school knew you won. That's not something not everyone knows."

"Alright, what they don't know is that I practiced every night in secret. I wanted to be known for something but I thought it would be better if they thought it was a natural ability."

Nat appreciated his dedication. "Why didn't you want anyone to know? Wouldn't they be impressed?"

"Maybe, but it was better for them to think it just came naturally to me. I don't know. Maybe it was dumb."

She reached out a hand and placed it on his forearm. "No, definitely not dumb."

He moved his arm so her hand slid down and his fingers intertwined with hers. "Your turn."

"I might've pushed for this excursion as an excuse to see you." The confession was deeper than she had meant to go when she first came up with the game, but it just slipped out in the moment of openness.

"I might've said yes to this excursion as an excuse to see you." He looked over at her for the faintest second, and Nat's heart melted. It was the perfect response.

Hudson

HUDSON AND NAT drove around a bit, looking for the perfect spot. They continued sharing little facts about each other. As the sun lowered, they had gone farther and farther away from the resort. They'd taken a short dirt road to a hilly hike that had the remnants of campfires dotting the land. Hudson thought it was too busy to be romantic. He tried a corner of the lake that had great views of the mountains, but it was too much in the open for winter. Then he thought about seeing how far he could push the Jeep by actually driving it up a slope. The death grip on his arm as he began to accelerate up a stony path made it clear he was taking things a little too far. As much as he loved winter, it was not giving him a whole lot of options for the Kents' date.

Soon, he had turned back toward the resort, and he could sense Nat's displeasure radiating from the passenger seat. She didn't seem upset with him, just disappointed that the perfect spot didn't seem to exist. But little did she know, he had saved one of the best spots he knew for last.

Just before the turn off to go into Hazel Oaks, Hudson pulled down a narrow side street framed in lush evergreen trees. At first, Nat didn't seem to notice his abrupt change in the original plan of heading back to the office to regroup. Then she looked up from the notebook she was writing in.

"Where are we going?" Nat asked, leaning forward in her seat.

"A buddy of mine is the sailing instructor for the resort during the summer. Do you know Finn?"

"I don't know him really well, but I recognize the name from the summer scheduling."

He was actually pretty pleased to hear that. All the girls seemed to fawn over Finn. He was a good-looking guy, if you were into guys who look like they could snap a tree in half and then build you a log cabin out of it. Not to mention the long dark hair, tan skin, and muscles you got from working with your hands every day. The idea of Nat hanging out on his boat filled him with an irrational pang of jealousy.

"Nope. I just send him his itineraries and sometimes he sends me an incident report if somebody does something foolish. I think I've only met him twice at company holiday parties."

"Well, he lives down this path and owns a bunch of land leading up to the lake. Before we left, I asked if he minded if we trespassed a little. He's out of town at some boat show, so we won't be bothering him."

"That's really nice of him. I know every summer everybody in my department gets worried that he'll get a better gig working in another resort or something. I guess it's pretty lucky he lives next door, so he can't escape," she said with a laugh.

"Yeah, he's a great guy. Anyway, he had me over for dinner last summer and there's this little river he showed me where he fishes sometimes. It's completely remote, and there's a dock he built out over it. I thought we could set up some chairs, maybe a portable firepit, and that would work."

Nat was almost bouncing in her seat at the mention of his idea. It warmed him inside to see the excitement on her bright face, and feel it almost bursting out of her as she squeezed his hand tighter. "Hudson, you're a genius."

He knew he probably should've shown her Finn's place first, but it was only a brief walk from the resort and an even quicker drive. And, to be honest, he hadn't wanted their trip to be over so quickly. Each new destination was just a longer stretch of time they could spend together, and after Nat's game in the car, he felt like every barren field and failed location was worth it.

Now they could sit on the dock and watch the end of the sunset when the stars first appear in the sky. Even better, she mentioned she brought a heated blanket for them to share if they got cold, and it was certainly shaping up to be a freezing evening. It gave him all the more reason to be close to her, something he was grateful for.

Moments of nearness made him want to experience that feeling of utter bliss mixed with fear and confusion as he looked into her eyes. Holding her in his arms was a feeling so completely grounding, that left him dizzy with the want of more of her. It seemed ridiculous that he had spent nearly two years at the resort and never realized how good it would feel to spend time with her. He wanted to remind himself that it was real and that it was a stronger feeling than he had ever experienced before. He still wasn't completely sure if everything about him lived up to her expectations of whatever romance was, but he sure hoped he did.

Really though, he was beginning to see just how futile it

was to stay away from her. The job in California seemed irrelevant as he drove, holding her hand, feeling the warmth coming from her, watching the excitement in her eyes. If he was honest with himself, it wasn't really a choice whether or not he had feelings for her. Whether he wanted to try to be with her. Fate seemed to have decided it for him.

Finn's house was an old one, not as old as the resort, but borderline historic. He knew a bit about the timeline, knew it was built sometime in the early 1900s and home to a few fishermen before falling into Finn's hands. Wooden, and white, it had a wraparound porch and a deep blue front door. Nestled within a forest of trees, one would never know it was beside one of the busiest resorts on the lake. The official Hazel Oaks's boats were kept on a dock closer to the resort during the spring and summer months, before being drydocked for winter somewhere unseen. But Hudson knew Finn kept his own small fleet for his personal use, and his winter business.

Hudson parked the car next to the porch and then went over to Nat's door, helping her down. He shouldered the duffel bag, then together, hand in hand, they walked from Finn's driveway to the river. As they walked, they continued their game, revealing more and more secrets to the other. Nat had just told him it was her dream to become the general manager of Hazel Oaks one day. She explained to him how much she liked the idea of staying in one place and having roots since most of her childhood was about moving.

"Don't you think you'd get restless?" Hudson asked as he listened to the sound of her heels against the newly poured pavement he hadn't noticed his last time at Finn's place.

"Not at all. It's my choice to stay here. Sometimes I think people are restless because they're lost, or they don't know what they want so they need to go and look for it. Once you've found what you want, I think it brings you a different kind of calm."

Hudson mulled over what she said. Unsure how he felt about her words and what they implied. Was he searching for something? Up until this point, he thought he moved around so much because he loved not having roots. But what was he searching for? Every time he moved, he looked for a job that would allow him to do physical things outdoors and then he'd go and find a gym. In reality, maybe he did have roots, roots that controlled what he did. Almost like a potted plant. They had roots, right? In the pot? He did the same thing and traveled around. Maybe that was the problem. He was still searching for something more.

Someone to love maybe? Someone like Nat? Maybe he was on the run because he never had anything, other than his family's insistence, holding him in one place. But would she be enough to hold him? More importantly, did he want her to be?

"I think you have a point," he finally said. "I moved because I could, since my childhood was pretty much spent in one location by threat of ex-communication from my family.

All the men for, you know, a million generations went to boarding schools of the military variety, so I had to. But now that I could choose to stay, I don't know. Maybe it's different. I've never really chosen to stay anywhere. I always feel like I need to move."

"Have you ever tried short trips? Break up the monotony?"

"Uh, no. I guess I haven't."

"Something to think about."

The trees began to grow farther apart as they neared the river. It was a narrow one, perhaps more of a stream, not that he really knew the difference. In the summer, he could smell a particular scent of fresh water and damp leaves that permeated the air. In the winter, all he could find was the ever-present promise of snow that never fell and the type of greenery that made him think of Christmas.

Soon, before he could start to worry about Nat's shoe choice, the dock came into view. The sun was barely able to guide them as he held her hand tighter, helping her down the slight slope to the river. He tried to picture how it would be once they joined forces to create another romantic moment. There would be a crackle of fire and a bubble of warmth surrounding them amongst the bitter wind that cut through the river's path, leaving the alcove of trees untouched.

"Views like that make you stop and think about what matters," Hudson said as they stepped onto the dock. Things were quiet, simple there.

"And what matters to you?"

He turned her toward him, taking her shoulders in his hands. He leaned down and placed a soft kiss on your lips. "Being here with you right now matters." He kissed her again, but this time, when they broke, the sun was replaced by thousands of stars above them.

"Hudson, I—"

He cut her off with a grin. "Just lie here on the dock with me and look up at the stars. I want to be still and take all of this in with you, your hand in mine. We can talk again in the car."

"But it's so cold."

He dropped the duffel bag and unzipped it, pulling out the blanket. "Here, it's all yours."

"Won't you be cold too?"

"Nah, I run hot." He sat down and patted the empty wood beside him.

Nat lowered herself, and he draped the blanket over her legs. Then he lay back and stretched his arm out so she could rest her head on it and then put his other arm under his own head. Her body heat helped him probably more than the blanket.

The sky was a brilliant smattering of lights, seemingly so near, but also so far away. They were stationary, remarkably so. For centuries, people had been plotting them, knowing exactly where each pinpoint of light would be on any given evening. Did they feel trapped? Did they long for something else, something different?

He wasn't sure how long they stayed like, that but he didn't want to look at his watch or his phone. He just wanted to imagine what it would be like to choose a home. And that was when he realized, he wasn't choosing a location, he was choosing someone who made him feel like home. With Nat, that was how he felt and that's what mattered.

They finally moved when he felt Nat shiver next to him.

"The blanket not enough for you?" he teased gently, turning his head to look at her in the darkness.

"I told you, I wasn't dressed for a lot of outdoors things. You know, we didn't even eat any of the food Terry packed for us, and that is so unlike you."

"What can I say, I was a little distracted. Why don't we grab dinner back at the resort? I know you're probably dying to check your emails anyway. How many do you think you have, five thousand? Have they sent out a search party because you didn't respond instantly?"

She giggled. "Oh, shut up."

Nat sat up and Hudson got to his feet before helping her stand. He stuffed the blanket back into the bag and shouldered it, then took her hand as if it were the most natural thing in the universe. The walk back was silent, but not the kind of strange silence he'd felt in the car earlier—the kind that didn't seem out of place between two people. He didn't think he had ever felt that way before, so completely anyway, despite what his usual demeanor would suggest. He had begun in his youth to use humor to disguise his pain and insecurities. Although he loved teasing Nat and seeing if he couldn't get her to smile just once, he also liked that he didn't need to put on a show, not anymore.

When they were finally in the Jeep and Hudson was making his way back down the road, Nat finally spoke. "Hudson, I think tonight might've been the most romantic time of my life."

He raised his eyebrows at her twice and smiled. "See, I told you I was good."

She swatted at him, but he caught her hand and gave her knuckles a kiss before driving them back to the resort.

CHAPTER NINE

Nat

THE WEEK OF Valentine's Day always sparked a rise in guests. It was nothing like the Fourth of July crowds or the Christmas crew, but couples came from all over for rustic, candlelit dinners and the chance for romance in a living snow globe. There would be flower deliveries, boxes of chocolates by the dozens, and a busy spa.

Nat flipped through the stack of papers on her desk and wished for another cup of coffee. Somehow in the midst of all her work with Hudson and the Kents, she had completely forgotten about a Galentine's Day group of girlfriends who were coming to spend a few days at the resort. They had their room, that wasn't a problem, but Nat hadn't exactly planned them the perfect itinerary. She hated having to delegate work to her staff at the last moment, but she didn't really have much of a choice.

She picked up her landline and dialed the number for one of the younger concierges, Rebecca. "Hi, I hope I didn't catch you at a bad time?"

"No, not at all."

"There is a group of four young ladies coming tomorrow morning to check in. I just need you to set them up with some spa treatments, a dinner by the lake, maybe something really fun with the adventure coordinating team, that sort of thing."

"No problem. I know you and Hudson are working on that big job, so I'll work with one of the other coordinators to set up some really fun things for them."

Nat leaned back in her seat, some of the tension between her shoulder blades lessening. "Thank you, Rebecca. I'll email you their information."

After hanging up and sending Rebecca a message, Nat stood up and stretched. She felt like she had been chained to the desk for the whole day. Normally, that wouldn't have bothered her. In fact, she used to feel perfectly at home in her little office. But since getting closer to Hudson, getting used to his constant presence and push for her to leave her desk every once in a while, she become accustomed to being a lot more active.

She forwarded her calls to her work cell phone and left her office to head to the kitchen. She completely missed lunch, half because she was busy sorting out last-minute Valentine's Day plans and half because she was almost hoping Hudson would come back from his hike that morning and ask if she wanted to eat with him. She didn't like feeling so clingy, but after spending that cozy afternoon together, then watching the stars, she found herself missing him a little. That feeling, she did like. They'd passed each other in the halls a few times since their outing yesterday, but they hadn't spent any real time together.

The resort was taking on the mantle of the holiday. There were no cheap cards or cartoon cupids in the lodge; she would never allow tacky plastic decorations to ruin the aesthetic of Hazel Oaks. Instead, the decor was subtle, understated and elegant. Red roses draped over the mantels of the fireplaces and in the guest restaurants, the same flowers have been placed on every table. There were small touches of gold here and there as well, mostly in the form of tiny golden heart-tipped arrows that had been hidden around the common spaces of the resort. When a guest found one, they could exchange it for romantic items, like a couple's massages, a private dinner, or cups of the special pink hot drinks in the cafe.

Hazel Oaks smelled of roses and chocolate, and the sight of couples holding hands and chattering to one another warmed Nat's heart as she walked the halls. Spending time with Hudson had made her soft. Usually, the Valentine's Day crowd excited her. It was always filled with couples showing her the promise of that deep love she longed for. Yet, it was bittersweet as she spent it alone year after year. For some reason, finding that meaningful date for this day always eluded her. She had to wonder if that was on purpose. Did she end things before Valentine's Day because she knew that person wasn't her epic love? She'd never considered consciously doing that. Now, she wasn't so sure.

This made her think about Hudson again, about their relationship, whatever it was morphing into. She felt chills flow through her body. Could he be the date to give her the same glow the other women had as they carried bouquets and held hands with their significant others? She hoped he did. There was nothing more lovely than someone in love. And then she stopped walking and froze. Love. Was she in love with him? She felt anxiety start to creep its way into her head. What did love even mean? Did it mean she no longer wanted to hit him over the head with her notebook? Did it mean choosing to spend time with him over anyone?

Nat leaned against the wall for a second, hoping the hallway would stay clear just for a few moments while she tried to figure out what her life meant and also why she chose to spend so much time in her office. If you have an existential crisis there, you can just close the door.

She'd once heard from a movie or a tv show that love meant they were the first person you thought of in the morning and the last one you thought of at night. But that could mean she was in love with Mr. Sutton. She'd certainly been thinking of him lately.

Nat didn't know if she had an answer right now. Did she love Hudson? She could make a list, some pros or cons list but if Hudson knew she made a pros and cons list about her feelings for him, he'd mock her endlessly and probably be a little hurt. Wasn't this supposed to be the easiest decision of your life? You find that person and you just know. Well, Nat didn't know. What did that mean? She didn't know if she did, she didn't know if she didn't.

She cleared her throat and stood up straight, adjusting her clothes. That was about all the privacy she could reasonably expect standing in the hall on the way to the kitchen of a busy resort. Honestly, that was probably way more privacy that she could've expected. Maybe there really was a cupid and she had her eyes on Nat. Now, if only cupid had an advice line she could call.

"Hey, you. Long time no see," Terry said as Nat stepped into her open office. "I feel like you haven't been in here in ages."

"Sorry, I've been so busy." She dropped into the chair across from Terry's desk. "How are things?"

"Just trying to make sure I don't extend my staff too much for the Valentine's Day dinners, or the big brunch. Then there was a mix-up with one of the suppliers, and for some reason they didn't send me a single potato. It's absolutely ridiculous."

"Is there anything I can do?"

"Can you deliver five hundred potatoes by tomorrow at six in the morning?" she asked with a grin.

"Unfortunately, I do not have any ties to the potato industry."

Terry lowered her voice and leaned forward on her desk.

"Then maybe you can deliver me some hot gossip?"

"About what?"

"About you and Hudson, obviously. I've hardly seen you, and when I do, you and he are usually sneaking off somewhere."

Nat's face flamed. "I told you we're working together on that project, but maybe we have been spending some extra time together."

"I knew it! You guys finally figure things out?"

"Yes and no. Mostly no. When we're not working, we have a lot of fun together, and I really like spending time with him. But it's not as if we've actually had a conversation about what's going on between us, or if anything at all is going on between us." She sighed and toyed with a gold bangle on her wrist. She debated going into detail about her earlier train of thought but Terry was just complaining about how much work she had to do. Nat couldn't monopolize her time. "You're busy. I shouldn't bother you with all this right now. I really just came in for some lunch."

"Oh no, you're not getting off that easy." Terry stood up and made for the door. "I'm fixing you a plate, and then you're gonna tell me everything."

"I didn't think you'd be so pushy, especially since me being busy means I'm not forcing you to run every night."

Terry shook her head and went into the kitchen, leaving Nat alone. She looked around the disheveled office, at the invoices on the desk and the few framed pictures that flanked the dark computer screen. There was one of the pair of them at an ugly Christmas sweater party three years before. She remembered staying up late that night gluing pompoms and bells to the ugliest orange shirt she'd ever seen in her life.

"Here, eat this and spill." Terry put a plated salad and a roll before her on the desk beside a glass of ice water. "You came in at such a weird time after lunch and before dinner. If you're still hungry when you're done, I'm sure I can whip you up something fast."

"No, this is perfect." She picked at the salad, not as hungry as she had been before in the face of telling Terry about Hudson. "Well, I'll just come out and say it, we kissed."

Terry clapped. "Took you two long enough. This is great news."

"Don't start planning the wedding just yet. I really want to ask him what's going on, but I don't know how."

"What do you mean? Boy meets girl, they like each other, they kiss, love. What's so hard to understand? You don't have to make a chart or a list to understand basic biology."

"It's not like that. Sometimes I feel so secure in whatever we have going on, and other times I feel like he still has one foot out the door," Nat confessed. "It's silly, and I'm probably overthinking it, but I can't help it."

"Then just talk to him about it. You're not going to get any answers until you two really hash things out."

She took a bite of her salad, trying to savor the raspberry vinaigrette. "You make it sound so easy."

"And you make it sound so hard. You guys can dance around the topic for the rest of eternity, or just come out and see that you actually care about each other. At this point, I should start taking bets with the staff on how long it's going to take you two to come clean."

"You wouldn't." Nat cracked a smile.

"Hey, Mama needs a new pair of oven mitts. Forget that, Mama needs a whole new oven."

Hudson

HE HAD BEEN standing in the lobby for the better part of half an hour, waiting to take Mina and Marvin to see the horses in the stable. Neither were keen on taking an actual ride but wanted to see the animals get some daily exercise in the paddocks. While not an exceptionally interesting outing, it was unlike them to be so late. At first, he thought he had the time wrong, but when he checked his schedule for the third time, he began to wonder if something had gone badly.

Did they have a fight since their last romantic date? Had Marvin said something foolish? Was Mina ignoring him? Were they in the middle of a shouting match in their room? The possibilities for disaster were endless, and Hudson began to panic. If things went poorly for the Kents, Nat would be an absolute wreck. She would totally blame herself, which he knew would be ridiculous, since Mina and Marvin were adults. Still, Hudson wouldn't let her do that to herself.

Deciding to not wait for the elevator, Hudson took the stairs two at a time. All the worst-case scenarios ran through his mind as he hurried down the hall to the Lake View Suite. Although he didn't hear any yelling as he approached the door, which he had to take as a good sign.

He knocked once, then again when no one answered, then a third time, beginning to worry. There was also a possibility they had left early, perhaps not even bothering to check out. Nat would have an absolute heart attack if that was the case. He pounded on the door again, giving it one last shot before he went down to the front desk.

The door shot open, revealing Marvin in a plush white resort robe. "Hudson, what in the world are you doing?"

"What happened? What's wrong?"

"Am I missing something? What has you all tied in a knot?"

Hudson raked a hand through his hair. "We were supposed to meet down in the lobby, but you guys never showed up for your appointment. I got pretty worried."

"Look, I know you and Natalie are supposed to be babysitting us, but we are twice your age and more than capable of amusing ourselves. You don't have to fill up all of our days with events and meals and facials." He had taken on a fatherly tone, the kind which was firm, but not angry.

"So, to be clear, you don't wanna see the horses?"

"No, Hudson, I do not want to see the horses. Come on, can't you see I'm busy here? Me and the wife are having a quiet afternoon." He gave him a pointed look and then took a step backward into the room. "Now, if you will excuse me, I have some time to kill before our dinner reservation. Maybe you should go spend some time with your girl instead of worrying about what I'm doing with mine. See you later."

He should have been pleased his time as nanny to the nearly divorced couple seemed to be coming to a close, but the end of that project meant the end of something else, he just couldn't place his finger on it. Maybe worrying about them had given him something to focus on for the first time in a long time.

He wandered back downstairs, now having a fairly free afternoon until he went to take the delivery of new kayaks for the spring and summer season. He could ask Terry for a second helping of the lunch he had earlier, maybe go over his maps a bit more, or find Natalie and see if she too had a free afternoon.

He hadn't seen her all day. His schedule had been crazy at the resort and then he'd had to hit the gym for a shift during his break. Ben said one of his trainers was out sick and begged for a little help. Hudson hadn't used his personal training skills since he'd left his last job in Colorado, but he had still managed to give the clients a good workout. In all that time, he'd been thinking about Nat.

Not wanting to go empty-handed, he went into the cafe

to get them both cups of that fancy pink hot chocolate all the guests loved so much. Just stepping foot in that room gave him flashbacks to slow dancing and tender kisses. It made his cheeks warm and his heart skip a beat.

He collected the two cups, two white mugs rimmed gold with a pile of frothy pastel-pink whipped cream, pink marshmallow hearts, and edible gold glitter stars. They looked a little much for his personal taste, but he had to admit the scent of the rich chocolate made his mouth water.

As he walked back to the staff offices, he wondered if bringing the romantic hot chocolate was maybe a little too much. Perhaps coffee or tea would have been more appropriate. But nothing about their interactions of late have been appropriate at all. Relationships between staff weren't forbidden; he checked himself in the employee handbook just the night before. But handing Nat a cup of Valentine's Day hot chocolate seemed to potentially give off the wrong impression. Although he wasn't quite sure what impression he wanted to give off.

He carefully knocked on Nat's closed office door, smiling when he heard her call, "Come in."

"Hey, I brought you a little afternoon pick-me-up." He placed one of the mugs on the desk in front of her, then sat down in the chair he once moved to her office, then never moved out. Instead of her usual red, she was wearing a tan skirt and jacket combo with a pink blouse beneath that brought out the color of her cheeks. And the bun she wore her hair knotted into didn't seem as tight as it normally did. Instead, a few tendrils of hair framed her face, giving her a soft look and making him want to brush them back behind her ear.

"Thank you, that is so sweet. I've been swamped today, so you are a lifesaver. Not to mention Nikki has been out all week with a stomach bug so I've either been here, or out in the welcome station trying to cover her shifts. And with Sutton and his wife coming, it's been crazy." She cradled the mug and inhaled. "Mmm, don't you just love how this smells? One of my favorite things about the resort this time of year is the rich sent. It's just flowers and chocolate, the perfect combination."

"I guess I haven't really noticed, although this drink does look pretty good."

"Have you never had it before?"

"Nope, can't say that I have. I'm usually not a huge chocolate person, to be honest."

Nat shot him a mock offended look and then sipped her drink. "Then you're missing out, I'm serious. This is delicious." She took another sip.

"Sorry, did you just say the Suttons were coming?"

"Yes, why?"

"Sutton is coming here? To check on us?"

"Oh, I told him about all the hard work you and I have been putting in, and he said he wanted to bring his wife here so they could experience some of that romance."

"Why didn't you tell me?"

Nat paused for a second. Initially, she'd intended to but she'd found out about their trip just before the two of them had that beautiful trip to Finn's and she'd been completely sidetracked. But she was being unfair; she should've told him. "I'm sorry. I should've told you. I meant to and I got distracted."

"See, this is what happens when you don't make notes in your all-knowing notebook. You make these kinds of mistakes."

"Really, you're making fun of my notebook?"

"You're gonna have to really pull it together if Sutton is coming. Can't be making these kinds of mistakes."

Nat rolled her eyes but smiled at him. His humor was starting to amuse rather than annoy her. Definitely a good sign. "I really am sorry. When I called his secretary to talk about plans, she'd told me his wife doesn't actually want to go on any hikes so I have them scheduled for things here. Don't worry, I'm not just gonna hand you a schedule with a hike with the Suttons and be like, surprise. Enjoy your day. I'd have let you know in advance."

"Then it's all good."

"Wait, weren't you busy all afternoon? You didn't cancel on anyone did you?"

"Have some faith, geez. I got canceled on, for the first time in ages. I was waiting in the lobby for the Kents and they never showed. When I went to find them, Marvin told me to kick rocks."

"Trouble in paradise?" She looked worried, and Hudson momentarily wished he hadn't said anything.

"No, the opposite. He told me they don't need a babysitter, that he and Mina were having a quiet afternoon in, then shut the door in my face."

"Then that's wonderful! They're spending time together without us orchestrating things, something they were both worried about."

"I guess you're right." He lifted the cup to his lips and drank, the whipped cream tickling his nose. It was hot and sweet, maybe a bit too sweet, but something he could certainly enjoy in Nat's company. "This isn't half bad."

"I swear, you have no taste."

"No taste for chocolate," he amended for her. "It just means you can have my share."

She reached over and plucked a marshmallow off the top of his whipped cream. "Don't mind if I do."

Her desk phone rang, and she gave him an apologetic look before answering it in her professional tone that was completely unlike the one she'd been using with him. Had she always sounded so casual with him, or was this a new evolution? If it was new, he wondered when it began. Was it a sudden change, something that happened all at once and completely? Or a gradual shift from coworker to something more?

That's what she was, wasn't it? She was certainly something more. He couldn't deny it any longer, even as he watched her taking notes in her little book as the person on the other line gave instructions. Every day they spent together brought them a little closer, making it difficult to imagine distance between them in the future. As alluring as California sounded, did he really think he would be alright with never sitting in her little office again or teasing her until she laughed that wonderful laugh that he found so infectious? He wasn't so sure anymore.

As soon as she was off the phone, he asked her, "Do you wanna get dinner tonight?"

To his surprise, she looked disappointed, then she said, "I'm sorry, I already have plans. One of my friends is moving and a bunch of us are getting together after work."

"Oh, that's cool. I was just seeing if you were free. But no worries."

She studied him over her cup and he looked down at his own, hoping she didn't see just how disappointed he was. But then again, he'd asked her last-minute. She had a life and it didn't involve waiting around for him to call. He should've done it last night or the night before.

"Hey, Hudson, how about tomorrow night?"

"Works for me. Leave from here, around eight?"

"Oh no, I'll starve. Let's make it six thirty."

"Six thirty? Are you sure it's alright for you to be leaving that early? Isn't that against the workaholics handbook or something?"

"Completely. But for you, I'm willing to break this one rule."

"Careful, Nat. When you say things like that, I get all sorts of excited. It's not fair to play with a man's heart the way you are."

"Somehow, I think you'll survive. Thank you so much for the drink, but I need to check in with Rebecca about a guest situation." Then she left the office with her mug, the fingers of her free hand trailing across his shoulders as she passed him.

Hudson let out a deep breath. He really had it bad.

CHAPTER TEN

Nat

HUDSON AND NAT spent the next few evenings together. They'd gone out to dinner, he'd taken her to the gym where, despite her fears, she didn't severely injure herself. She was actually in great shape. They also had a movie night in. Each time he left her, Nat was more and more hopeful the initial seeds of romance would soon bloom. They had a connection that she couldn't quite explain. On paper, they didn't make any sense. In fact, they were polar opposites, but maybe that's why they did seem to work.

The day before Valentine's Day, Marvin sat in Nat's office. She was excited to see him since he'd been pretty absent since shaking off Hudson's last attempt at getting the pair to go out with him. The Kents had canceled all of their premade adventures, with the exception of dinners, and asked for a rental car for more freedom. They'd even declined the sunset date at Finn's house, requesting they have more privacy. Frankly, Nat was glad not to be babysitting anymore, because she'd always felt a little weird about chaperoning people older than her parents. But then again, it'd gotten her and Hudson to see different sides of the other.

Marvin tapped the arm of his chair, the rhythmic sound one of excitement, not stress. "Natalie, first of all, I am so grateful for everything you've done for Mina and me. Truly, this trip has been a much-needed wake-up call about the state of our marriage. We've done a lot of talking and we've come to a decision about how to start off on the right foot. Tomorrow, we'd like to renew our vows."

"What? Oh Marvin, that's just, that's amazing." There was nothing she adored more than a happily ever after, and she was thrilled to bits she had helped them find theirs again. Then the reality of their timeline hit her. "Pardon me for just a moment, but did you say tomorrow?"

"Sure did. Mina and I want to have a little ceremony here with George and Ellie, and our daughter is coming up as well. We're just thinking something small with a casual meal after."

Nat's mind started whirling. Nearly every romantic spot inside the lodge had already been reserved for romantic dinners and small events. Even the greenhouse was booked for a morning proposal.

"Marvin, I'm not sure we can squeeze something like that in on such short notice. We could maybe set something up outside, but the weather can be unpredictable here."

"I know it's last-minute and I know it makes more work

for you, but you've really changed things for us, and I know you can do it. Whatever the cost, the fee, whatever, I'm more than willing to throw some cash around to give Mina a perfect time. This is the place that brought Mina and me back together and, obviously things aren't perfect, and we're clearly still going to have to work on a lot but that's what this vow renewal is about. It's about promising to do that. We even have a couple's counselor ready to help us at home. We're going to make this work."

Nat flipped open her planner and skimmed the packed day. If they could make it work, then so would she. There were slivers of time where she could possibly fit something small in, but not enough to do a room turnover or serve a full dinner. But how could she say no to him? "I'll work something out."

"Excellent. Just tell the wife and me where to go and we'll be there." He stood up, shook Nat's hand, and then headed out of the office.

Nat drooped in her seat, not caring if her skirt wrinkled. What was she going to do? She started making a list of all the things she'd need and at the top of the list was break the news to Terry that she'd have to squeeze in another fabulous dinner. She doubted he actually meant casual. And even if he did, she wanted it to be special for them. Though telling Terry, that would actually be the most dangerous part of all this. A location was vital, but she'd need to have a talk with the whole team about where to hold the ceremony and meal.

Then there was the decor, the officiant, maybe even a cake?

There was a knock on the frame of her open door. She looked up and saw George Sutton standing there with his trademark toothy grin. She put on her best customer service smile and stood to greet him.

"No, no, Ms. Keller, back as you were. No need for formalities."

"Alright," she said, dropping back into her chair. "Well, welcome back to Hazel Oaks, sir."

He eased into the seat opposite her desk. "Thank you, thank you. Now, I've just seen Marvin and I have to say, a vow renewal? You and Hudson must've really worked your magic. Did you find a cupid to help you out?"

Nat laughed her melodic customer service laugh and waved her hand at him. "Of course not, sir. We all know cupid doesn't exist. Actually, Hudson and Terry have worked tremendously hard on this project alongside me, and I'm very proud of their ingenuity and dedication. And Rebecca, one of the stars on my staff, she took up a lot of my slack while I focused on the Kents. It's really been a team effort."

"Yes, naturally. You have a fine team here. I've been meaning to ask you, this team, is there something I can do to show my gratitude for them?"

Nat thought about Terry for a second. She's been begging for a new oven for quite some time, and Rebecca had planned to have her wedding at the lodge when she saved enough. She quickly mentioned these things to Mr. Sutton and he took out his phone to make notes.

"Easy enough. Tell Terry to send you the oven that she wants, and we'll work on getting that for her. As for Rebecca, that would be my pleasure. Tell her the rental fee will be on me and we'll give her a thirty percent discount on catering when she's ready to book."

"That's all so generous of you, sir."

"All your work has been generous, and Hudson, is there something I can do for him?"

Nat opened her mouth and closed it again. She knew what Hudson wanted as well. He wanted that job in California. But if she said it, he'd leave. If she didn't, she'd be selfish. She couldn't ruin his career like that. Besides, if he wanted to move, she didn't want him here, right? She wanted a man who would move mountains to be with her, not just climb them when they were trying to bring a couple back together. She could argue with herself for days about what the right thing to do would be, but in the end, she couldn't deny Hudson's true wish of leaving Hazel Oaks behind for the land of sun and surf.

"Hudson is eager to move to the California property, the Jewel of Laguna. He's mentioned being an adventure coordinator there a few times, and I think he'd really appreciate having a chance at a position."

"Splendid. He'd probably do well there. Tell him to send me his resume and I'll personally pass it along to HR."

"Great," she'd said, but she felt her smile crumble. This was one time she couldn't fake it.

"And you, we can't forget about you?"

She nearly told him all she wanted was a little more time to figure out if things with Hudson had a real shot or if he might stay with her, but she shook her head. "Nothing for the moment, sir. Can I get back to you?"

"Absolutely, you have my cell." He stood up and straightened his tie. "And also, Natalie, I know Marvin wants a vow ceremony, but I had a thought on that. Do you have any of the suites open?"

"There are two of the junior suites open, but I don't think they'd be big enough for the ceremony and the dinner. I just—"

"Oh, I agree with you. The wife and I will move to one of them for our stay. My personal suite is certainly large enough to accommodate the vow renewal. We just arrived, so we haven't even unpacked. I can have one of the front desk staff move us so you can get started."

"Mr. Sutton, that is fantastic. That does make things a lot easier moving forward."

"Then my job is done." With that, he turned and walked out of the office after shooting her another wide grin.

Nat knew she needed to start planning for the vow renewal, but she also knew she needed a minute or forty to pull herself back together or she was in danger of becoming completely overwhelmed. She called Rebecca and told her she needed to step out for about an hour. Then, she went to her car and got her running clothes. If ever there was a time where she needed to escape her thoughts, it was now.

Hudson

HUDSON SPUN HIS office chair side to side as he read over an incident report. One of the guests had fallen during a hike with one of the junior coordinators and hurt their ankle. Everyone present had insisted it was an accident, and that's how the report read, but Hudson just wanted to make sure everyone was alright before closing the case. He called the guest to check on him but his wife said he was sleeping. She said the hospital said it wasn't broken so he was just sore.

When he finished, he headed to the kitchen for some food. He needed a late lunch before he had to lead a couple to a sunset proposal. The plan was to take them to the wishing well, which one of the groundskeepers had cleared, just in time for a wish and a ring. He even charged up the resort's camera so he could take some good photos for a keepsake. But first, sustenance.

He strolled through the lobby looking at the vases of flowers on just about every flat surface. Valentine's Day wasn't exactly his thing. He'd never really celebrated it with someone and just used the day after for a change to restock his candy collection at home when everything was on sale. But now with Nat in his life, he was trying to figure out what he could do. He talked a big game to her about how he was a king of romance, but now with his own Operation Valentine ending as a success, he had to think of something fresh. Though, he wasn't above asking for a little help.

"Terry," he called when he entered the kitchen, which was still buzzing with post-lunch activity as the staff cleared for dinner prep. "I simply cannot get through another minute without your cooking."

Terry came out of the walk-in freezer, holding a clipboard. "Why can you never come during the hours we serve lunch to the employees? We have a cafeteria for a reason."

"Because I enjoy this one-on-one time with you...and I was dealing with a hurt resident who needed a trip to the hospital."

"Seriously? Are they okay?"

"Yeah, their ankle wasn't broken, but you know how I loathe paperwork."

"Alright, I guess that's a good excuse for today. I'll get you something." Terry put the clipboard on one of the empty counters and washed her hands. Then she walked to the fridge near the back of the kitchen and started pulling ingredients out for the world's best sandwich. There was ham, turkey, lettuce, tomatoes, some bacon probably from breakfast, honey mustard, mayonnaise with olive oil, and pickles.

She started to assemble the sandwich, humming quietly to herself. Hudson watched her work after getting himself a drink from the fridge, trying to think of an opening. He wasn't great with verbalizing his feelings. He'd basically been raised with drills, silent meals, and clean-cut order. And opening himself up like that wasn't something he was wildly comfortable doing. But like with bungee jumping and paragliding, sometimes you just needed to take the leap.

"Listen, Terry, I also wanted to talk to you about Nat."

"Oh yeah, what about her?" she asked without looking up from her work.

"Is she really into Valentine's Day? Like should I do something big or small or should I ignore the day completely since this is all still new?"

Terry turned from the sandwich and placed a gloved hand on her hip. "I am not telling you how to seduce my friend."

"What? Terry, mind out of the gutter. I just…forget it." He took a long drink and stared at the finished sandwich she pushed in front of him. He didn't want to tell Terry he'd never had a date for Valentine's Day. Not a real one anyway. She'd definitely tell Nat and that just felt weird for her to know.

"Are you really asking me this? Like you really want to know?"

"Well, yeah, who else would I ask? You know every-thing."

She twisted the lid back on the mayo, beginning her cleanup while speaking. "Okay, then I'm ready to be serious. Nat does everything for everyone. She's obsessed with organization and structure, right?"

"Yes."

"So, give her a fully planned-out date she doesn't need to worry about. Show her you put effort into it. She knows how much it takes to set up that stuff, and she will appreciate it for that reason. It doesn't have to be this big expensive event, just something thoughtful."

"Okay, so nothing cliché, more like an act of service?"

"You got it."

"You're right. I got this." And he turned to walk out of the kitchen, eager to check his schedule to see when he could devote a few hours to setting something up.

"Uh, Hudson," she called after him. "Your lunch?"

"I don't deserve you in my life," he said, giving her a gentle kiss on the cheek as he took the proffered plate.

"Yeah, yeah, yeah, say it in chocolate."

"Done!"

Hudson's head was swirling with ideas. First, he wanted to plan something for the fifteenth and not on Valentine's Day. She had a full day of activities between romantic brunches and spa treatments, so she'd probably be exhausted. Maybe that would be the first thing he'd take care of for her. He could go to one of the fancy boutiques in town and get her some bubble bath soap stuff and maybe some candles and more notebooks. That would be a good place to start.

He was so deep in his thoughts he almost ran straight into Nat in the lobby. Luckily though he held on to his sandwich.

"Sorry, deep in thought," he said smiling at her, but she didn't smile back. In fact, her eyes were a little puffy. Had she been crying? "Hey, what's wrong?"

"Um…nothing…actually, can we go talk in my office?"

His stomach flipped. "Talk, like, I'm being sent to the principal's office or talk like you want to share whatever is bothering you?"

"Just follow me, please." She turned and walked straight down the hall toward the offices, not even looking behind her to see if he was there.

Hudson took a big bite of his sandwich, preparing for the worst. He was pretty sure he hadn't done anything to upset her. They'd been getting along perfectly for weeks and he thought they were having a great time together. He was ready to do whatever he could to fix this. It had to be terrible. She didn't even have her customer service smile on. At that moment, he wanted to do anything to ensure she never felt like that again. Obviously, that was impossible, but he didn't care. He'd try.

He sat across from Nat in her office, holding the sandwich awkwardly in his lap. He should've tossed it out before he walked in, but he had been laser focused on trying to sort out where things went wrong. And the look on her face had completely taken away his appetite.

"Nat, you're freaking me out. What's going on?"

"It's actually a good thing," she said, trying to smile. But she couldn't get it to reach her eyes. It didn't even brighten her cheeks.

"A good thing for who?"

"For you."

"Is this when you tell me I have a deadly disease, but it's alright because it's operable?"

She frowned, seemingly taken aback. "What? How would I know your medical history?"

"Nat, what's going on?"

"Two things. One, good work with the Kents. They're renewing their vows here, which is great. Two, I talked to Mr. Sutton today. He is really pleased with the work we've done with the Kents. He asked if there was anything he could do for you, and I mentioned your desire to go to California. Mr. Sutton said to send him your resume and he'll pass it on personally to the resort's human resource team."

Hudson didn't respond. He wasn't exactly sure how to. One word from Mr. Sutton meant he was leaving. Leaving when they'd just started talking, seeing each other, whatever it was they were doing.

"Nat, I—"

"Isn't it exciting?" she asked cheerfully. It was false, sharp, but it looked like she was committed.

"It is, but I thought you and I—"

"No, don't, Hudson. This job is what you want. It's what you've been talking about for weeks. You're leaving and I get it."

He wanted to reach across the desk and take her hand but couldn't move. "Nat, I didn't even apply for the job yet. I haven't said I'm leaving."

"I know but you will. Just make sure to give me two weeks' notice so I can fill your role."

"And which role is that, boyfriend or adventure coordinator?"

Her gaze, which had fallen to the folders on her desk flicked back up. Her expression was unreadable as stone. "You were never my boyfriend. We never got to that point. I thought we could've, but it's clearly not in the cards. If you'll just excuse me, I have a vow renewal to organize." She grabbed her usual notebook and headed out of her office like there had been a fire alarm.

Hudson stayed in his chair. He wasn't sure how to process what just happened. Going to California was what he wanted and then it wasn't. With Sutton sending his resume out, it was a guaranteed job, a straight shot to the life he thought he was working toward. But it was also the end of the life he had in New York. He'd be leaving Ben and the friends he'd made at the gym, and the other adventure coordinators. He'd never eat Terry's food again, and he'd have to say goodbye to Nat just when he felt he'd really gotten to know her. And here he was, planning this romantic Valentine's Day thing for her. It felt wrong to do any of it now.

She was right. Their entire relationship was new. They'd wasted so much time being annoyed, irritated, or frustrated with the other. While he had friends in California who never made him feel like he was breaking the rules. Friends he'd wanted to help. He tossed the sandwich in the trash and then dropped his head in his hands, running them through his hair. This was a mess. He needed to talk to somebody. He called Ben and asked if they could meet up when he finished work. Someone needed to help him sort out the rest of his life.

CHAPTER ELEVEN

Nat

N AT ADJUSTED THE ivy draped over the fireplace's wide, cream mantel. Leafy tendrils framed the flickering fire, carefully fastened out of the way by invisible hooks. On the mantel itself sat tall white candles that waited to be lit. There were more candles on the white draped table that had been brought in for the dinner service following the ceremony. She'd spoken to Mr. Sutton once more before setting up the event, asking him question upon question about the Kents first wedding.

It was true to its time with bridesmaids in rusty orange and disco music at the reception. She had decided to modernize the feel with sunset shades of roses on the table and a bouquet of the same shades for Dr. Kent to hold. The tech team had set up small speakers throughout the room, which was originally the suite's living area. She'd had it completely emptied in preparation for the party which meant she had plenty of space. Rebecca had compiled a list of songs encompassing the years they'd been together while Terry's team served their dinner, an updated version of their first wedding feast. There would be fondue to start, then some salmon and an assortment of vegetables, followed by a Black Forest cake for the couple to cut.

For only being put together in less than a day, everything was falling perfectly into place. Even Terry hadn't complained when Nat came to her with a menu idea based on a dinner from decades long ago. Although the promise of new kitchen equipment would have gotten her to be excited to cook just about anything. Rebecca was similarly thrilled at the prospect of saving so much money on her dream wedding.

Hudson was the only one who didn't immediately cheer when Nat laid out the deal she'd made on his behalf. She had been replaying the look on his face for hours. She hadn't expected him to be anything less than perfectly thrilled. With the promise of his dream job, she'd thought he'd look just a little pleased. Instead he'd dropped a bombshell on her she still hadn't quite gotten over. He'd called himself her *boyfriend.*

Nat rounded the dinner table and went to the balcony doors, which were similarly draped in ivy. The balcony for Mr. Sutton's personal use was much larger than the other guests, with a perfect view of the lake from the top of the resort. A pair of heating units had been brought up, as well as comfortable chairs so the party could move outdoors for a nightcap beneath the stars.

She leaned on the smooth, wooden railing and took a deep breath of the cool, crisp air. It was like she could hear that word on the air, *boyfriend*. The breeze cut straight through her suit jacket, but it felt good against her fevered skin. It was nice to focus on something instead of her thoughts. She was getting so tired of being trapped within her own mind.

But as she watched guests milling through the garden maze below and strolling along the half-frozen shore, she felt terribly alone. Her parents lived close by and she spoke to her brothers every week. She saw Terry every day at work and her close group of girlfriends was always there for dinners, brunches, and movie nights. In truth, she wasn't completely alone, but she was missing that special brand of togetherness that only came with being part of a couple. An official one.

Nat had been so sure this Valentine's Day would be different than the last. She had hoped for a box of chocolates and a nice dinner, or a bouquet of flowers delivered to her office like some of the other women received. The idea of a faceless man taking her out on the town for Valentine's Day had been replaced with Hudson's cheeky grin and teasing ways. He was such a secret romantic, and she was eager to see what he'd be like for Valentine's. But now, she just wanted the day to end. In fact, she was thinking about taking a vacation. She had days saved up, and it'd been forever since she'd gone. Maybe that was just what she needed, some sun, a good book, a tan...and space. She'd come back from her vacation with a fresh perspective, and then saying goodbye to Hudson wouldn't be so hard.

She'd gotten so used to having him by her side the past few weeks. His infectious laugh and the way he'd managed to pull her out of her orderly shell had changed her. It wasn't a purposeful thing, not a complete push toward being some-one new, but a gentle nudge into living a more balanced life. She had spent more evenings having fun than thinking about spreadsheets and timetables. She'd gotten better at asking for help and seeing things through his eyes, visions of perfectly imperfect disorder that always ended up magical.

When she had begun to plan the vow renewal, Nat al-most asked Hudson to help, but thought better of it. If he was going to be gone soon, she needed to start separating herself from him. She had to stop looking for him when she heard footsteps down the corridor, or her cell phone buzzed with an incoming text. It would be hard to keep him at a distance inside the lodge, but it was the first step in making sure she didn't get too hurt. It's what she'd always done when her dad's orders changed. She'd start pulling away from friends, claiming she needed time to pack, and then, when she actually moved, it was easier. After a few weeks, it wouldn't hurt to contact her friends, to check in, to maintain that friendship from a distance. It would work with Hudson too.

"Nat?" called Rebecca from inside the room. "You still

up here?"

Nat left the balcony, closing the door securely behind her. Rebecca was pushing a cart stacked with gold framed photographs. Each one featured pictures of the Kent's lives over the years, sent to Nat by their grown daughter who was over the moon her parents had decided to give their marriage another go. They were just snapshots of their lives, wedding pictures, family photos in front of the Christmas tree, vacation shots at Hazel Oaks, slivers of their history.

"These came out so nice," Nat said as she began placing the photographs on the mantel and end tables, nestling them between the roses.

"Didn't they? I was waiting for them to be delivered all morning and was starting to get really worried."

"It looks like everything's falling into place."

"They are going to love it. You and Hudson make such a good team."

Nat paused, her fingers just touching the framed snapshot of the Kents on a cruise. "This was a team effort. You played just as much a part as we did. We all make a good team."

"Hey, it wasn't me having late-night dinner meetings with you," Rebecca teased as she straightened the gold event chairs framing the table. "Don't get me wrong, I'll take the credit, but it's really nice to see you and Hudson together."

"We aren't together, just working. I'll keep that in mind for next time I work on a project, make it clear it's all professional."

"Professional, right. That's not what I saw the night of the salsa lessons."

"Easy to confuse things when you take it out of the office. I was just trying to fit in and make the Kents happy. That's the mission, right? Keep the customers happy."

"Whatever you say," Rebecca said in a singsong vice.

Nat shot her a small smile and picked up some fallen petals from the floor and placed them in the garbage can. "I think we're actually done here. What do you think?"

"I think it looks beautiful. Really. I wasn't sure how I was going to feel with the ivy and the orange roses, but for some reason it really brought it back in this vintage sort of way."

"I'm sure the florist can recreate the look for your wedding."

Rebecca wrinkled her nose. "I already planned on lilies."

Nat and Rebecca left the suite with Rebecca heading to the elevator with the cart and Nat taking the stairs. There was romantic piano music playing in the lobby, and the space smelled of flowers and rich milk chocolate. Floral arrangements were being wheeled in by a delivery man, boating bouquets of everything from birds of paradise to daisies. The atmosphere was delightful, despite the pain she felt in her heart, and a genuine smile touched her lips as she descended the steps.

Mina was at the concierge desk as Nat passed and waved

her over as she collected a garment bag. "Oh, Natalie, I can't tell you how thrilled I am that you managed to put together our vow renewal. I know it was such short notice, and I felt so terrible about putting more work on you, but Marvin was insistent that you would make everything beautiful."

"It was nothing, really. I just hope it lives up to your expectations."

Her eyes shone with tears. "You've really worked some Valentine's Day miracles, and I'll always be so grateful to you and Hudson. I didn't think we'd make it this far, really. To think, I almost didn't want to come. And now...now Marvin and I are getting a second chance. I still cannot believe it."

"I always knew it would work out, and tonight will just be the next step toward the rest of your lives."

"And you and Hudson will come, right?"

She shook her head with a smile. "No, this is a private event just for you, no chaperones required."

"I didn't mean as chaperones; I meant as guests. It's only fair you attend...although I suppose asking a young thing like yourself to give up her Valentine's Day hardly seems fair. You've already done so much and I'm sure you have plans."

In truth, she wouldn't have minded attending the vow renewal to see all her hard work end with a bang, but the idea of sitting at the miniature wedding next to Hudson put her stomach in knots. "I've set up a photographer, so I'll see all the pictures."

"Alright, well, my dress for tonight was just delivered, so

I'm going to go hang it up before the pampering begins."

"You received the salon itinerary I sent with breakfast this morning, right?"

"Sure did. I have to say, the salon and spa are two of the things I'll miss the most after going home," she said with a wistful look. "Nothing makes you feel twenty years younger like a facial and a blowout."

Nat waved her off as she headed toward the elevator. Then she soaked up a bit more of the good feelings and promise of romance the lobby held for everyone who passed through.

Her office though was another matter, bland and boring, unfulfilling for the first time since she first placed her name card into the small frame on the door. She normally adored being behind her desk and making orderly lists, but after sweeping through the romantic lobby alive with music and blooms, she couldn't help but long for more color and life.

She undid the French twist her hair was knotted into and massaged her scalp. Playing cupid for everyone else was certainly fun, but after her confrontation with Hudson, she found it difficult to melt into the rest of the day's plans. Still, there were dinners to oversee and an evening proposal in the study to set up, so once she made a few calls, she'd have to get back to work. She twisted her hair back up and then reapplied her lipstick. It felt like a shield. Right now, that was what she needed.

Hudson

HUDSON PASSED BY Nat's office three times that day, always finding the door closed. He hadn't seen it shut since before Operation Valentine was in full effect, and she was in the habit of holing away with her lists and orderly notes. Every time he passed, he considered knocking and seeing if she was alright, or pushing her to talk about California, but his fist always paused before it hit the dark wood.

His chat with Ben the night before at the gym hadn't gone as planned. When Hudson had explained how his desire to date Nat was at war with his desire to go to the Jewel of Laguna, Ben had just told him to follow his heart. What Ben didn't understand was that life wasn't an animated kids' movie where it always ended with a happily ever after since all the right choices were always made. Real life was messy and the choices weren't always clear. And besides, he didn't know what heart to follow.

In the end though, he had to admit Ben was right. Whatever decision Hudson made, he was going to have to live with it, for better or for worse. No matter what he chose, he was going to give something up, either his dream job or Nat. Although his dream job would probably be just as temporary as any of his other gigs, with him maybe moving on in a few years to something new. But then again, wasn't that the dream?

There was no stability in Nat either, not that he could guarantee anyway. They could date for years and then break up, never speaking again. But if that happened, he'd be stuck in Hazel Oaks until he could find another job. The problem was, that new job, it might not be all he wanted. Though, if he were honest, he'd taken crappy jobs before to get out of town. Not that it was ideal but it kept his wheels moving. Both choices were a gamble and he didn't know which card to play.

After the sunset proposal at the wishing well, Hudson had wandered back outside after depositing the newly engaged couple at the resort. He didn't want to walk past Natalie's office again and see the door shut to him or bump into her in the hallway. He had the feeling she didn't want to see him, since she apparently hadn't thought to tell him about the Kents' vow renewal, outside a brief email saying she had it in hand, and it was a private ceremony so his presence was not needed. It worked just fine for him though, since he needed to think without seeing her. Or maybe it was something else. Maybe he was scared to see her.

Hudson pondered this as he wandered through the perfectly landscaped maze. If he saw her, what would he say? That was probably why he couldn't knock on her door. He'd see this beautiful and accomplished woman in front of him and all logic would rush from his brain. Instead, he'd be left wondering how he could ever imagine leaving someone like her. His life, his actions, they'd never felt tied to another human like this before.

Hudson went and sat on one of the patio chairs that surrounded the fire that seemed to never stop burning. It wasn't empty, but with everyone being coupled up, they didn't spare him much more than a glance and a smile as he sat down, which worked just fine with him. He had a lot of thinking to do.

Planting roots had never appealed to him, even as a teenager when his teachers and guidance counselors would ask what he wanted to be when he grew up. He could be basically anything he wanted, he had the connections and the job history to ensure it, but in truth all he ever wanted to be was free. He didn't mind having structure at work where he had bosses to answer to, but he still felt he didn't have the same sort of chains working as an adventure coordinator.

He tried to picture himself at Hazel Oaks in one year, three years, five years...he always seemed to be living the same life. Of course, he couldn't see the future, but he could see the stability in it. He would still be pestering Terry to be his personal chef and discovering new little pockets of the world like the wishing well. And he and Nat would share coffee in her office between appointments and try out new restaurants after work. He could be comfortable there, so predictable and easy. But would that predictability start to feel like a collar tying him down?

When he tried to imagine what living in California

would be, he was sure it would be fun for the first year or two as he helped build up the gym and swapped his hiking boots for diving flippers. But that was it. The good seemed to have trouble outweighing the negative. He'd give up the clean Lake George air and the regular guests he'd grown close to. He would have new coworkers, new challenges, a new adjustment period where he would be the new guy again. Sure, he'd make friends at the gym and there were all kinds of Spartan competitions up there. He'd never run out of things to do or interesting people to meet.

And then there was Nat, orderly, structured, beautiful, witty Natalie Keller. He'd wasted a year not knowing her and only recently realized there was so much worth knowing he could spend a lifetime learning about her past, her future plans, her hopes, her dreams, her fears, and never get to the bottom. He would miss her bright red lipstick and the easy way she opened up when she began to trust him. Not hearing her melodic laugh or sharing plates of fried food again seemed so trivial, but in reality, it was nearly unthinkable.

Hudson didn't want to go so far as to say he was in love with her, but was there another word for what he was thinking? Adoration seemed too old-fashioned and infatuation too impermanent. Obsession was a little stalkery and didn't seem appropriate.

Things had moved quickly, just how he liked them to in every other aspect of his life, and he didn't mind with Nat.

He liked her, really liked her from the bun in her hair to the click of her shoes on the tile in the lobby and from her sharp retorts to the gentle silence that surrounded her when she stood on the shores of the lake. She had this depth to her that he loved to explore. Life in Hazel Oaks may have been pretty predictable but time with her wasn't.

The one thing he wasn't completely certain of to his marrow was if she felt the same way. If she had, wouldn't she have said something when he mentioned being her boy-friend? Or kept her mouth shut about the Jewel of Laguna resort when Mr. Sutton asked what Hudson wanted? Maybe that was her way of getting rid of him now that their project was over. Or worse, testing him. Girls did that kinda stuff, right? Then he shut that idea down. Customer service Nat would never deny him a job she knew he wanted. She had her business suit on. She was way too considerate to hold that offer from him and risk it affecting his life.

The empty chair beside him moved with a scrape. The junior adventure coordinator Jordan had sat down, a grin on his face.

"You look pretty happy," Hudson said in greeting.

"I could say the opposite of you, but I'm in too much of a good mood to let whatever is bothering you bring me down."

"Well, aren't you a good friend."

Jordan laughed. "You know I'm just messing with you. Did the couple you took out for the proposal break up or something?"

"Nope. It went off without a hitch and I have the pictures to prove it."

"Then care to share what has you looking like that?"

Hudson stared at the flames, remembering the saying there were two things in the world man could look at that was both always changing, yet never changing, fire and water. "I did so good with that older couple, you know, the one who were about to divorce, and I think I'm going to get a spot at the California resort."

Jordan clapped him on the shoulder. "Congratulations, I know you were really looking to get in there."

"Yeah, it's pretty great."

"If it's so great, why do you look more like you just got fired?"

Hudson debated laying it all out for him, but it seemed inappropriate. Jordan was a great guy and he liked hanging out with him sometimes but dropping his problems with Nat on his shoulders wasn't right. "Just have a headache. I always forget how busy it is on Valentine's Day."

"Tell me about it."

"You were working with that group of girls, right?" Hudson asked, eager to change the conversation to something else.

Jordan's grin was back, and he leaned back in his seat. "Yeah, the Galentine's Day party. Working with them has been a blast."

"You never seem this excited about your other guests."

"Things are a little…different this time."

"Different how?"

"There's this girl, one of the ones that came with the group. We ended up hanging out a bit and I really like her."

"Look at you, a valentine."

"Hardly, the group's leaving tomorrow, and who knows if I'm going to see her again. Long distance just isn't my style."

Hudson grimaced. The conversation was back to making him think about Nat. "What if you really liked her? Like, you knew her for more than just a week or so? What would you think of the distance then?"

"It depends. I don't think I'd be much good for long distance, but if I really cared about somebody and I wanted to make it work, I'm sure I'd figure it out. I'm a romantic like that." He let out a deep sigh. "I don't know, man. It's like if that girl can make me feel like this after a week, I'd be pretty excited to see what it would be like to be with her for a month, or a year, you know? It's a crazy ride. I just wish it was the right time."

"How do you know it's not?"

"Thanks for listening, buddy, but yeah it's not our time. I feel it. You know when you can just feel it, down somewhere in your gut? I feel it's not the right time. But, man, if it was another time, it would've worked."

They sat in silence for a few minutes, taking in their own

thoughts. After a few more minutes Jordan said he was going inside to warm up some.

Hudson sat by the fire much longer than he meant to. The other couples had drifted off to dinner reservations and bed. Still, he let the flames warm him as he periodically added more kindling and logs to keep it going. He promised himself that he wouldn't leave that spot without a plan one way or the other. He would either formally put in his two weeks in the morning, or try, truly try, to make Nat his. Was it their time or was it just a moment in time? Either way, he was in for a long night. One thing was for sure, this decision couldn't wait until after Valentine's Day.

CHAPTER TWELVE

Nat

N AT TRUDGED INTO work late that day, just after lunch. The Valentine's Day rush had taken everything out of her, and by the time she'd gotten home to her little apartment, she basically fell into bed and into the deepest sleep she'd had in a while. Her exhaustion had been a positive, since she couldn't exactly think too hard about Hudson and her own disappointment about the day.

Every time there was a knock on her office door, or someone called her name, she expected him to be there. She wasn't sure what she thought he'd say, if it was to give his two weeks, bring her a Valentine's Day card, or maybe even tell her he was staying at Hazel Oaks. But as the day wore on, it was clear they weren't crossing paths for a reason, and she knew she'd just have to come to terms with things being strained between them.

After her usual email check, she went to see Terry for an extra-large coffee to perk her up. The lobby still held the remnants of the holiday, though the flowers were a bit wilted and the music no longer played. But there was still the distinct feelings of love and adoration she'd soaked in the day before. Even the couples were more reserved, quietly checking out to leave the small bubble of romance the lodge provided. She hoped they all had been touched in the same way the Kents had.

The kitchen was calmer than it had been in days, though still full of pre-dinner activity. The scents of roasted potatoes, chicken, and whatever delicious soup was boiling in the massive pots all smelled amazing. She was glad she came in late so she would be able to take advantage of dinner later, but until then, should make do with the large coffee she got herself before stepping into Terry's office.

Terry was sifting through a pile of papers with a pen tucked behind her ear, but looked up and smiled when Nat came in. "Hey, stranger, I was surprised I didn't see you bright and early this morning."

"As if I could after yesterday," she said as she dropped into an empty seat. "It seems like we get more and more couples every year."

"You say that like it's a bad thing."

"It's not. I'm just exhausted."

"I can tell. Looks like your outfit wasn't ironed within an inch of its life today."

Nat looked down at her black cigarette pants and red sweater. It was certainly way more casual than she usually was, but she wouldn't be interacting with any guests that day and took a chance at being comfortable. "You don't like it?"

"I never said that. I'm glad you're not in another pant-suit. It always makes me nervous to feed you something messy, in case you spill. I don't want to rack up a dry-cleaning bill."

"For your cooking, that's a risk I'm always willing to take."

"Are you hungry now? I can make you a plate of something."

"No, I'll wait for dinner. I'm not sure what the menu is, but I know I want to take full advantage of it."

"Not sure you'll be able to make it to the cafeteria to-night," Terry said as she pulled the lid off the pen and made a mark on one of the papers.

Nat's blood ran cold for a moment. Had she forgotten something she scheduled? Her daily planner was sitting on a drawer in her office. She stood up, leaving her coffee on the desk. "Oh no. I had no idea I had an appointment tonight. I have to go figure out what I—"

"Wait, you didn't forget anything, I promise."

"Then what's going on?"

Terry smile, her eyes sparkling. "Well, you do have an appointment, just not the kind you're thinking of."

"I'm totally lost. Will you just spit it out already?"

She slid a file over, revealing a large cream envelope that read *Natalie* in black letters. She handed it to her, looking rather pleased with herself. "Here you go."

Nat turn the envelope over, looking for any sign as to who it might be from. "What is this?"

"Hey, I'm just the mailwoman, not your secretary. Open it up."

"As if you didn't read it."

"I have no idea what you're talking about."

Nat slipped her finger beneath the fold and ripped the top of the envelope. She recognized the cardstock within, fine and silky, the same kind she'd given Marvin to use to invite Mina out for a night of dancing. Then she began to read.

Dear Nat,

You once said a handwritten note was the more romantic way to ask someone to spend time with you. I realized I'd never written you a note, although all I want to do is spend time together these days. If you'd like to spend time with me, go to the guest garage at 4:30.

See you soon,
Hudson

Nat looked back at Terry. "What's going on?"

"What do you mean what's going on? He's doing some romantic gesture for a late Valentine's Day. Come on! Go, have fun, let me live through you."

"No, no, I'm not doing this. He's leaving for California, and I'm not starting something just so I can say goodbye. I'm done with that nomadic life."

"Do you have his two weeks?"

Nat looked at Terry and felt like all air from her body

had escaped her. "He's going to give me his two weeks on Valentine's Day?" she shouted, letting the entire kitchen hear her. It would be like he was quitting their relationship and the resort at the same time. "I'm not going."

"Alright, so that took a different turn than I was expecting," Terry said. "I just mean, go and see what he says. Maybe he isn't leaving."

"He's leaving."

"I'll believe it when you have his two weeks' notice in your hand. That boy is falling in love with you."

"Maybe. But he's already in love with California. I'm not enough."

"Stop." Terry slammed her wooden spoon against the counter. She stuck a pointer finger in Nat's face. "Listen to me. You cannot see the future and you certainly do not actually control everyone in this building. That man cares about you. Anyone here can see that and you will not speak badly about my best friend. She is always enough. If he goes to California, it won't be because you aren't enough. It will be because he wasn't ready for all that you have to offer. But you have to let him decide that. You can't do it for him by avoiding him or whatever it is that has the two of you looking like you do. Now, it's almost four thirty. Get your butt to the garage and then call me afterward because I'm spending my night cooking and not with a dreamy man staring back at me."

Nat left the kitchen without another word, and she hurried back to her office for her coat. She pulled it on along with her gloves and her favorite gray scarf. Then she forwarded her office calls to her cell phone out of habit and headed outside. The garage wasn't too far of a walk, and the afternoon seemed fairly mild for February. She was wondering what she would find there. Would it be Hudson handing her his two weeks' notice? The thought made her stomach dip. He was always a jokester, but she didn't think he would be so cold as to lure her into something like that with a note.

To her surprise, Jordan was leaning against one of the open bay doors, spinning a set of keys round his finger. "Hey, you made it."

"I guess so. Where is Hudson?"

"At the next location." He reached inside his jacket pocket and passed her an envelope.

"Let me guess, you have no idea what's written in here?"

He shrugged. "Just the messenger."

"We need to establish a rule about reading other people's messages," she grumbled and then opened it up.

Dear Nat,

If you're reading this note, that means you've decided to give me a chance tonight. I had no idea what your reaction would be to the first but I'm grateful you made it. Follow the map to the next destination. I promise it's not a trap.

See you soon,
Hudson

Nat turned the cardstock over to see a rather well-done, hand-drawn map. It gave clear instructions up one of the mountain paths she was familiar with. She could see it led straight to the greenhouse, which overlooked Lake George. But a hike like that would take some time and when she put on her black booties that morning, she hadn't planned on traipsing up the side of a mountain.

"Jordan, does he really want me to go mountain climbing right now? I would need to go change."

"No need. I know you know how to drive one of these bad boys." He tossed her the keys, which she nearly dropped in her surprise. "Those go to the red quad in the back."

Nat had never been gladder to have not been wearing a skirt that day as she tucked the cards into her coat pocket and tightened her scarf tighter round her neck. The drive would only take ten minutes and the sun was still out enough to keep the paths bright. Though her nerves made her hands shake. She hated the unknown in all its forms.

The air was brisk, biting at her exposed cheeks as she drove, her hastily done braid loosening with every mile. It was a bumpy ride, though she tried to dodge potholes and keep to the middle of the path. But soon she recognized the turnoff that led to the greenhouse, half hidden by an outcropping of rock.

The greenhouse was a hidden gem of Hazel Oaks—built sometime in the 1920s for one of the Suttons who oversaw the lodge—all in crystal-clear glass supported by perfectly aged green metal; it had withstood the test of time. The rose bushes within always flourished in the balmy heat, even when there was snow on the ground and the temperatures dipped below freezing on particularly bitter nights. She hadn't gone up there as much as she wished, and she wondered what was waiting for her within.

It sat on the clear outcropping, which had been kept clean of brush and stones to trip over. And the doors faced the lake in the beginnings of the sunset. She took a deep breath before reaching for the handle to pull it open. Once she did, she was engulfed in the delicious aroma of hundreds of roses in full bloom. Red, white, pink, yellow, they grew in a multitude of shades and hues that welcomed her inside. Honestly, she should come up here more often. It didn't seem like a bad place to think.

But she couldn't focus too hard on the flowers when Hudson was standing in the center, dressed in a pair of well-worn jeans and a blue sweater that brought out his eyes. She instinctively wanted to go to him. But she wasn't sure if that would be the right thing to do. If he pushed her away or moved to California, she wouldn't know what to do with herself.

"I'm glad you came," he said in a very soft, un-Hudson like voice.

"How could I not?" Her heart was beating so loudly, she felt he could hear it. Was he using this as an elaborate way to say goodbye? It would be the most beautiful goodbye she'd ever had. Maybe that was why he did it, to give her one more special moment for them to share. If that was the case, she'd cherish it.

"Really, I wasn't sure if you would. Here, let me take your coat."

She shrugged out of her jacket and accessories, but with them she also felt like she was somehow giving him her armor. Like she was stripping away any kind of wall she'd put up trying to brace her heart for the end. But she still turned them over, ready, deciding in that moment that whatever would happen, she'd handle it with grace and try to hold on to a smidgen of her dignity no matter how much it hurt.

Hudson draped her things over one of the two white wrought iron chairs framed a small table she hadn't noticed before. There were covered dishes that reminded her of their salsa evening, and she knew Terry had a hand in whatever was going on.

"Hudson, what am I doing here?" she dared to ask.

When he didn't immediately respond, Nat feared she'd made a grave mistake.

Hudson

HUDSON DIDN'T LIKE the tone of her voice. She sounded

wary, nervous and flighty. It was completely unlike the confident Nat he hoped would meet him there. But he supposed he couldn't blame her too much, since he had been an absolute wreck waiting to hear the gentle roar of the engine coming up the mountain. Though, he had a feeling Terry would've gotten Nat up the mountain if she'd had to carry her. Still, Nat was always the collected one and here she was, all raw emotion. It unnerved him.

He bridged the gap between them in three short steps and took her hands in his. Despite the chill outside, they were warm inside the greenhouse. He loved seeing her surrounded by roses. They brought out the pink in her cheeks and the streaks of red in her hair. If she let him, he would bring her here all the time.

"Natalie, I wanted to talk to you about California."

Her hazel eyes widened, and she tried to pull away from him. "I accept your two weeks' notice."

"That's too bad, because I'm not giving it. I've made a decision, and it's really important to me that you're the first one here to know exactly what it is." He bit the inside of his cheek as she blinked away unshed tears. He had never been great with words, but this was getting completely out of hand. "Nat, I talked to Mr. Sutton today. I didn't take that job. I'm not moving to a new resort. I'm staying at Hazel Oaks."

Her lips parted in surprise. "But...but why? I thought you really wanted that job."

"I did, but Nat, I want you more," he admitted, pulling her closer. "I couldn't imagine myself being so far away from you. The job in California is just that, a job. I have one here. I'm paying my bills and get to do what a love. I've been given a lot of freedom here, and I feel like I'm not done yet. California isn't right for me."

"But, Hudson, you might not have that opportunity again."

"Why? Do you think I couldn't get an amazing job in California in the future if I wanted to?"

"No, of course you can, that's not what I mean. I just—"

"Nat, listen to me. I called my buddies in California with the gym and set myself up to be a distance partner. I'll fly out there every few weeks or so for large events, but that's it for now. And then I called Mr. Sutton and made a new deal."

"What is it?" she asked in a breathless tone.

"I told him I wanted to stay here at Hazel Oaks and ex-pand the outdoor obstacle course and bring in a new type of guest, the kind of Spartan athletes I get at the gym. Then I'm going to be consulting on the other resorts' adventure programs if the courses pan out like I think they will. I can't leave you. I just feel in my gut that this is right."

She pulled her hands free of his and threw her arms around his neck. He followed suit, holding her close around her middle as the deepening sunset poured into the green-house. She hadn't said anything about his announcement, but he didn't care. All he knew was that she was in his arms and that's where he longed for her to stay.

Finally, Nat looked up at him, a smile finally on her face. "Do you mean it, Hudson? Are you really staying?"

"I am. Are you happy about it?"

"How can I not be? It takes so long to train new adventure coordinators."

"Haha, very funny." He cupped her cheek, silencing her with a kiss. "We did just start, and I'm not ready to end it. I got a taste of what it was like having you in my life and I didn't want to give that up."

"But you gave up California."

Snow fell against the panes of glass, a gentle flurry that glittered behind the roses. "I didn't, not really. I thought I constantly needed to keep moving. If I kept moving, then it meant I wasn't tied down and I was free. And then I realized, what's the point of being free if you feel required to move? No, I'm free because I'm choosing to stay. I'm choosing you."

"I choose you too, Hudson."

The End

Want more? Check out another Sarah and Kelsey sweet romance, *Falling in Puppy Love*!

Join Tule Publishing's newsletter for more great reads and weekly deals!

If you enjoyed *Operation Valentine*, you'll love the next book in the....

Hazel Oaks Resort series

Book 1: *Operation Valentine*

Book 2: *Coming soon!*

Available now at your favorite online retailer!

If you enjoyed *Operation Valentine*, you'll love Sarah Fischer and Kelsey McKnight's other sweet romances!

Royally Abandoned

Cupid Claus

Falling in Puppy Love

Available now at your favorite online retailer!

More by Kelsey McKnight

The What Happens series

Book 1: *What Happens in the Highlands*
by Kelsey McKnight

Book 2: *What Happens in the Ruins*
by Kelsey McKnight

Book 3: *What Happens in the Castle*
by Kelsey McKnight

Available now at your favorite online retailer!

About Sarah Fischer

Sarah Fischer works hard fighting the good fight in personnel security. She graduated with a degree in criminal justice and married the calm to her crazy. Then Sarah had a health scare and needed heart surgery. While recovering, she finally had the time to write the stories playing out in her mind.

Her college romantic suspense series, Elton Hall Chronicles, is now available in its entirety on Amazon. First Semester, Second Snowfall, and Third Wheel remind you what you loved about college, show you what you missed, and make you yearn for what could have been. Sarah also has a contemporary short story in the Craving Bad anthology.

In her spare time, you'll find her with a book in her hand, at the movies, or watching just one more episode of reality tv.

About Kelsey McKnight

From Scottish lairds to billionaire businessmen, Kelsey McKnight will ignite your soul, no matter what century it lives in.

Kelsey is a university-educated historian from southern New Jersey. She has married her great loves of romance, history, and literature to create her own tales of dashing heroes, sultry bad boys, and lovable heroines who have their own stories to tell. They will take you through the ballrooms of Victorian London, the hills of the Scottish Highlands, New York City penthouses, and into small towns with big hearts, all at the flip of a page.

When she's not writing, Kelsey can be found reading, drinking too much coffee, spending time with her family, and working for a nonprofit organization.

Thank you for reading

Operation Valentine

If you enjoyed this book, you can find more from all our great authors at TulePublishing.com, or from your favorite online retailer.

TULE
PUBLISHING

Made in the USA
Coppell, TX
06 February 2021

49720874R00166